FORBIDDEN AND EXPLICIT EROTICA FOR ADULTS:

9 Extremely Taboo Stories

VOL.3

by Rebecca Sin

I would like to invite you to read another one of
my books that I think you will really enjoy.
The book is called:

***"BDSM DARK SEX:8 Unraveled Explicit
Stories For Adults VOL.2"***

Enjoy!

This is a work of fiction. Names, character, places and incidents are either the product of the author's imagination or are used fictitiously, and any resemblance to actual persons, living or dead, business establishments, events or locales is entirely coincidental.

@ COPYRIGHT 2020
by Rebecca Sin

FIRST EDITION 2020

Table of Contents

THE OFFICE SLUT
Office Anal Story

I'm really quiet a shy man, not one for chatting up the girls in the office. The flirting is sort of fun, but I never know what to do after the first few times. And then I see the light die in their eyes, and the conversation goes safe and boring.

I do talk to them, but I hear about their boyfriends, families, domestic problems and holidays abroad. Never anything personal, never any hint about what they think about me.

I was married once, lasted 5 years, if you can call a slow falling apart a marriage. She was the first girl I slept with who seemed to enjoy herself. I was so grateful I proposed to her. I know, not a good basis for a marriage. And anyway, as I said, she only seemed to enjoy herself. After a while I found out that she had been scared of being on her own, and really she wasn't that interested in sex.

I work in an office, sort of the second-in-command of the department. It's open plan and I have a desk by the aisle to the coffee machine. Without having to be too obvious, I can see a lot from here, but at the end of the day, I'm too much of a coward to do anything about it.

Anyway, last week this new girl started, well woman really – she's over 25, and not giggly and silly like the younger ones. Mind you, I don't suppose most men notice whether she giggles. She has a figure you could fry an egg on. Her tits bounce in her blouse like a couple of puppies fighting in a sack. And her bum; what I wouldn't do to see that naked over my lap. I have seen her smile, (I can look up you know), and I've caught her looking in my direction and smiling at me. I suppose it's because we're both a bit older than most of the staff who are mostly school-leavers fresh from 6th form.

She sits over the aisle from me, facing me. We can see each other and smile, but conversation would mean standing up and going over to her – far too scary.

And talking to her? I'd be so tongue tied I'd need surgery to loosen it up again. Somehow, I can believe that this woman doesn't just like sex – she lives for it. I bet she's got some big biker boyfriend or a trucker for a husband. Some male chauvinist jerk that gives her a right seeing to twice a week, and doesn't really appreciate what he's got.

So, she starts last week, and on the first day I stop by her desk and introduce myself (I'm a polite little bugger really). Her name is Chantelle, and she has cool soft hands. Apart from that, standing in front of her looking down the front of her blouse, I got vertigo. I could see this silken valley, and the lace fringes of her bra. I moved away before I ended up drooling down her tits. Well, now she knows who the shy boy in the office is.

Anyway, that was last week. You can tell she's settling in. Most of the guys have stopped by and had a look see. She's friendly, but not too friendly, I like that. And when she catches me looking in her direction, she gives me a cheeky grin and a little wave – just between friends.

She's also started dressing a bit more relaxed. Her skirts are getting shorter, they're mid thigh now, and her heels are getting higher. And her blouses? I could swear they have been shrinking in the wash, and have fewer buttons. One thing I have noticed, though, she wears hold ups. When she sits down, sometimes the skirt rides up a bit, and I catch a glimpse of the banding where the elastic grips the thigh. Lucky elastic, her thighs would look so good around me.

Today, however, feels different. There is a new intensity in Chantelle. It's like she has made up her mind about something. Whatever it is, some lucky bastard is in for a treat. You know what I said about her blouse shrinking? Today it's so tight she hasn't bothered with a bra. Her tits look softer, but still have a wonderful shape and I itch to touch them, rub them, and chew the little nubbins at the tips. I can see her nipples clearly now, casting shadows on the whiteness of her blouse. She must have someone in her sights, and she's brought out the big guns.

Earlier, I heard her voice a bit louder than usual, talking to a client on the phone. I glanced up, and did a double take. She was leaning back in her chair, looking at the computer screen. Or at least, her face was looking at the computer screen. Her body was facing me, and her legs were wide apart, her heels on the ground. I could just make out this flash of red, in the gloom at the top of her legs. Bloody hell, I was looking up her skirt, and she was making it easy for me. I looked away before she caught me ogling her. When she put the phone down I looked again, and she gave me a big smile and a wink. As I said, some lucky bastard.

A few minutes ago she dropped her pen, the third time this morning. As always, she has to lean forward and I get a □uick look down her blouse. This is killing me. It's like she's got what I want and she's dangling in front of me, like a treat for some poor puppy. I wonder if she really knows what she's doing to me.

What's this? She's sent me an e-mail.

"Richard. Would you mind helping me later? I have a

report I need to present to Mr. Jones tomorrow, and I am stuck on the spreadsheet calculations."

I don't need to be asked twice. Quick mail back.

"No problems Chantelle. When time would be good for you? I am free from about 3:00pm onward."

"That's so kind of you. I have a lot to do this afternoon. Would you mind staying late?"

I think to myself. Would I mind staying late with the delightful Chantelle? Does a dog lick its balls?

"Not a problem Chantelle. Why don't we say 5:00pm?"

Because of my grade, I have the keys to lock up in the evening, so no-one would be surprised to see me staying late.

"Thank you Richard. I'm ever so grateful. Chantelle xx"

Whatever hot date Chantelle is going on, she doesn't seem to be in that much in a hurry to get there.

The day drags, the clock playing silly buggers and dragging

its heels around the dial.

I'm seriously looking forward to working with Chantelle. Just the chance to sit next to her, to smell her, to imagine what dirty things I could do with her. I clamp down on that last thought quickly. You're out of your league Ricky Boy. She would eat you for breakfast, and feed the pips to her pet budgie.

It's 5:00pm. Some people are already leaving, and I know they'll all be gone by 5:30.

I look over at Chantelle and catch her eye. I raise my eyebrows as if asking a question, and she gives a smile and a nod. At the same time she starts to clear some papers away as if making room.

Trying to look relaxed and casual, I wonder over, and swing round the chair behind her so that I can sit on her left.

"So tell me, what's the problem."

"Thank you for helping me Richard." and she gives me a 140 watt smile. "It's these "If, Then" commands. I want to have blank cells where there aren't any answers apart from zero"

I run through formulae on Excel, and then how to construct the particular one she wants. She nods in understanding. This has taken 15 minutes, and the office is now completely empty apart from us two.

I then ask her to show me the sheet she is working on. Once it's up, I lean across her to take charge of the mouse.

She puts her left hand on my right thigh. I freeze.

I look at her, and she smiles, giving me a wink. Shit - I'm the lucky bastard she's been gunning for. I look at her, too stunned to speak.

"I'm sorry Richard, but I couldn't think of any other way to get you on your own with me. You see, I'm a really naughty girl, and I have been hoping you would notice and do something about it."

"Errr, like what?"

I know, stupid question, but I can be a bit slow at times.

Chantelle doesn't seem fazed by my hesitancy. She draws little patterns on my left thigh with her finger – leaving burn marks on my skin.

"Well sir. You could spank my bottom. And then I would be truly grateful. Very, very grateful in fact."

All my dreams have come true. All my fantasies have distilled themselves into this wonderful creature beside me. She wants me to do what I have been itching to do since I first saw her. I lean back in the chair, shock making me bold and adventurous.

"Too bloody right you are a naughty girl. All those slutty outfits. All that showing off your legs to me. And now this, lying to get me on your own with me. I really do have to spank your bottom for that."

Bless her, Chantelle looks grateful, and I watch her smile with happiness. I am certainly getting this one right.

"But first, I want you to stand up, and take off your skirt. I want a bare bottom to spank – no fabric in the way."

Without a word, She stands up and faces me. Slowly she pulls down the zip on the side of her short skirt, and she lets it fall, stepping out of the crumpled circle on the ground.

She is wearing a bright scarlet thong – just a thin scrap of lace coving a hairless pussy, with the two strings around her hips and one diving between her thighs. One zip, and we're down to bedrock.

"You tart. You're dressed for a whore-house, not an office."

Chantelle blushes, but does nothing to hide the evidence of a slow leakage from her cunny.

I stand up facing her.

"OK, punishment time. Turn round, bend over and put your elbows on the table. I'm going to give you ten spanks, five on each cheek.

She bends as requested, and I am rewarded with a tight bubble butt presented for my hand to work on.

And the second shock of the day.

Normally, a thong slips between the creases of a woman's bottom, rubbing her anal ring like a naughty finger.

In this case, there is a purple disk pushing the string out.

I reach out and touch it.

Bloody hell. She's wearing a butt plug. She's come to work dressed like a whore, wearing a fucking butt plug. This is awesome.

"You dirty, sex mad little girl. You're wearing a sodding butt plug."

She nods. In a little girl voice she speaks up, her head on her arms.

"I know sir. Is that really bad sir? Are you going to punish me even more sir?"

I pull down her thong off her hips, and the musky scent of her excitement fills the air.

"I was only going to spank you ten times. But as you have this disgusting thing in your arse..."

And at this point, I reach out and twist the plug. I am rewarded by a gasp, her stomach pulling in and her hips bucking.

"I am going..."

Another twist and a moan. "To spank you..."

Twist and groan.

"Another.... ten....times."

At each word I give the plastic implement buried in her arse another savage twist. I can tell the stimulation is driving her crazy, and there is more juice down the inside of her trembling thighs. Chantelle starts babbling.

"Oh God, please sir. Please spank me sir. Do it hard and make me cry sir. I'll be a good girl and I'll suck your cock. You can fuck my cunt sir, as hard as you like.

If you really want, sir, you can shove your thick cock up my arse and make me take it like a proper slut until you fill me with your wonderful spunk."

She really knows how to reach me, and her words are music to my prick, which is now banging on the inside of my trousers, screaming to be let out.

I spit on the palm of my hand, and measure up the distance.

The crack of flesh on flesh echoes in the empty office.

Chantelle whimpers, and rolls her hips.

"Stand still cunt, or I'll tie you down.

"Anything you want sir, please just do it."

With a measured pace I deliver the first ten blows - finding some clear space free of redness each time. Her wide arse is reddening nicely, and I am mesmerized by the way the flesh bounces on impact, but returns to its position with a blush on its cheek.

I pause, for my hand's sake. I can hear muffled sobs from Chantelle, but her bottom is still thrust out, and she has made no effort to cover it or stop me.

I slide a hand between her thighs, and reach in to inspect the ripe fig of her hairless sex. Liquid is pouring from the slick entrance. The punishment might be hurting her behind, but it's also making her cunt hot.

I slide my left hand under her blouse and place it on small of her back, pushing it down. Before she can work out what I am about to do, I deliver ten more blows. These are much more rapid, more stinging than hard, and are delivered five to one cheek then five to the other.

This flurry of blows is like one long rumble of thunder to her bottom. The intensity of the pain on her already tender posterior grows, and with it her own climax. As the last shocks reverberate, her orgasm hits – triggered by the onslaught.

I stand, in awe, as I hear her wail of submission, and her hips jerking as if fucking some imaginary stud. Her fingers reach down to her sex and rub hard to increase and prolong the rolling waves.

She stops, her fingers buried in her wet twat, slowly pumping in and out, her breathing ragged.
"Oh God, thank you sir. That was wonderful. Please fuck me now sir. Do what you want, I am all yours."

I stand behind this embodiment of every wet dream I have ever had. Her dark hair is lying tousled on the desk. Her head is resting on one arm while her other hand slowly frigs her cunt. Her thighs are apart – joined near the top by the thong pulled away from her two fuck holes. And nestling in her red raw cheeks, a large purple anal invader.

I don't really have much choice.

I reach out and untwist the plug from her. She whimpers as

the head stretches the raw ring of the entrance. I toss the rubber bung onto the table, and step up to the breach, which is slowly clenching shut. There is still enough lubrication from the plug's insertion to allow me to force my way in without too much difficulty.

Pausing only to line myself up with her back door – I push myself in as hard as I can. She's a pain slut, and she's already stretched. She screams out a loud "Yes!!!", and then I am buried deep in her colon, my thighs pressed against hers.

I love traveling the chocolate highway, it's so perverted and she looks wonderful bending over taking it. To my surprise, she reaches behind and pulls her cheeks apart, giving me a better view of her ring being hammered in and out, sucking my cock like a tight hard mouth.

This isn't going to be a marathon session – she is egging me on with her filthy slut language, promising me even more depraved fun if I will only cum in her arse. She tells me how much she loves this, dreams of this, begs me to do this every day, and promises to lick my cock clean with her wet mouth every time I have finished.

And all the while I am lost in the hot, silken shit hole of a woman who is giving my cock the ride of its life, grunting with pleasure at each hard thrust in and clenching withdrawal out.

All too soon, the top must blow. I Quickly thrust in two more times before I have to stop to feel my spunk rippling up my cock and spurting into her dark hole. I am crying out with happiness and a fierce joy.

Chantelle is again furiously rubbing her empty cunt, and joins me as I unload my cum in her. My cock feels like it is about to be ripped off me, so hard do her muscles spasm and her body shake with the climax. It feels bloody wonderful, and I can hear her cries of release.

When I stop to catch my breath, Chantelle collapses, spent with the two massive orgasms. True to her word, though, she slips to her knees, and engulfs my exhausted cock in her lapping mouth. She looks up at me naughtily as she does a thorough cleaning job.

And then it hits me. I may be the Office Shy Boy, but I'm the one who has just fucked the Office Slut. And from the way she is performing – it won't be the last time.

CANDY AWAKENING
First Time Anal Story

Dave and I had been married for eight years when he gave me an erotic novel. He had bought me the little short stories but this book was much larger than those were. I didn't want to seem too anxious to read it, so I made myself wait for a little while. I am an avid reader and the idea of a purely erotic novel had me excited so I finally gave in and kicked back to read.

It didn't take long at all to discover that the main character, a woman named Candy, loved anal sex above all sex. It seemed that the bigger the cock the more she wanted it inside that "other hole".

In our marriage, anal was discussed loosely, almost jokingly. I had told my husband at that time there was no way that I wanted any part of that. Dave had said that it was ok and unnecessary but I couldn't help but wonder, "Is the anal sex story a hint to convince me to try it out?"

In my reading, I fully admit that I found it intriguing. Until reading it, I really hadn't given anal sex more than a passing consideration. Now, it turned me on to think that it could be that erotic. Candy spoke of an intense fullness, a pleasurable pain beyond anything ever felt during "real sex".

I've always enjoyed the pleasure pain of real sex. The feel of someone deep inside pushing against the deepest part of my pussy and here was this story where it hinted that "back there" was even better.

I read a little and being thoroughly turned on, I went for my vibrator. In seconds, I came simply from holding the vibrator on my clit while reading. That book brought me off several times during the few days that it took to read it.

It wasn't until I finished the book that I decided I wanted to feel all that Candy had felt. I wanted to try anal sex and it wasn't easy for me to admit to that, even to myself. I couldn't imagine mentioning it to Dave. He had already said it wasn't necessary and even after eight years of marriage I still had to wonder if he would think less of me for saying that I now wanted it.

Worse yet was the idea that if I said I wanted it to go there, what if I couldn't handle it? I wasn't sure what to do about it.

A few months later, the book and the anal sex stuff still filled my mind. I had yet to mention it. I've always been rather shy about stuff like that. I don't want to be the one to suggest new things to anyone. The book wouldn't go away though. Experiencing anal sex became my number one fantasy.

I often grabbed the book and brought myself off while reading it. I envied Candy and her love of anal sex. I couldn't picture the feelings she described in her sexual encounters but every time I read, I wanted to feel it more. The pleasure pain of it, the overwhelming fullness that it gave her, filled my mind.

There was also the amount of fooling around that she described as necessary. I wanted to be teased mercilessly until I was begging for a cock to be inside me, anywhere. I wanted to have a man in my rear hole and have him reach around and massage my clit.

I thought about it long enough until one day, I decided that rather than tell Dave that I wanted it and then not be able to go through with it, I would try it out on my own first. Then if it was more painful than suggested by Candy, I could easily back out and no one but me would be the wiser. I wouldn't have to tell anyone that I had tried it and couldn't make it work. Either way the "Not knowing" would be over with.

I grabbed a toy that was both long enough to hold on to and

a little smaller around than Dave, a bottle of lubrication that we always kept around, and my book of Candy's adventures. I started out just reading. I started at page one and probably read a few chapters before touching myself. Even though I had already read most of the book twice, it could still turn me on very □uickly.

By the end of chapter three, I was more than ready to put a vibrator on my clit that would send me over the edge. That wasn't what I was aiming for this time though. I didn't want the quick release offered by a vibe on my clit.

I stood up beside the bed and finished taking off my clothes and then I got down on my hands and knees on the bed. Candy seemed to use this position often, even when she chose to play solo. I figured that it would probably work best for me as well, especially because it would allow both my hands the freedom to be where I needed them.

I read a little more, using the vibe on my clit a little bit, but not enough to bring myself off. I wanted to wait. I wanted to be ready for anything that I might feel, pleasure or pain.

I read another chapter in the book, and came very close to cumming. I decided it was time to stop playing and go for it if I was going to and before I lost my nerve or became so turned on that I simply couldn't stop myself.

I slid the vibrator back toward my rear entrance and enjoyed for a moment the feel of the vibrations back there. I had felt it before but knowing what I would be doing soon made it even more exciting.

I teased myself that way for a little while, and now I was really wanting to cum. I didn't want to waste a whole lot more time with the build up. Curiosity was winning and I needed to see what it would feel like to have something inside me.

I took the vibrator and put lubrication on it then rubbed it around again. I did this several times making sure that my ass and the toy was coated very well with lube. I then reached for the night stand beside the bed to get a bullet vibe for use on my clit once the vibrating cock was inside my ass.

I turned off the vibration on the cock, wanting to make it easier on myself if possible and I began slowly trying to push it into my ass. I was glad that I had chosen a toy with a very small point and a gradual slope to full size around.

At first, my ass didn't want to let it in, so I pushed a little harder and tried to make myself relax. That was very hard to do considering I was scared it was going to really start hurting at any moment.

I'm not sure if it was just the fact that I was pushing it in firmly or if I was able to relax enough to let it in, but the toy cock finally managed to get inside me a little bit. It did hurt, but it wasn't horrible. It was a very uni☐ue pain, coupled with the satisfaction of knowing I was making this happen. The toy wasn't inside very far at all but I still wanted to squeal in happiness over the fact that I had got that far with it.

I held the toy still and moved the book back to where I could see it easily. Candy was just beginning another sexual encounter. I read through it and as the man in her world pushed his cock inside her, I pushed the toy cock further inside myself.

The man in the story paused when he was balls deep inside her and let her adjust and I held still with my wrist against my pussy and the toy cock as far inside me as I felt I could possibly handle. I felt and can say with reasonable certainty that I took all but a couple inches. I wasn't sure if I had made a right choice in either picking a toy or wanting to go anal at all because it was hurting, but at the same time, I felt so full that I didn't want to stop.

After a few minutes of allowing myself to adjust to that new fullness, I started reading again. I moved the toy cock in and out of my ass slowly. I wasn't able to pick up speed with the couple in the book but I continued to read while moving it in and out of myself slowly. When they were finished and she went to clean herself up, I discarded the book, anxious to bring myself off. Even though the discomfort was there, I was growing more and more turned on by it.

I pulled the vibrator out of my ass, but only long enough to add a little more lube to the mix, and pushed it back inside myself. It didn't hurt as bad the second time around and I was both amazed and happy about that.

I laid my head down on the bed, leaving my ass up in the air and really began moving the vibrator in and out again. As my arm bumped up against my pussy, I could feel the wetness of myself and wondered if it was from the lube or just because I was that turned on.

I moved it in and out of myself for a while and just enjoyed the feel of it, the naughtiness of what I was doing to myself. With every stroke of the toy, I was becoming more desperate to reach orgasm.

I reached for the small bullet vibe and turned it on high and placed it between my legs and centered over the top of my clit. I couldn't believe the overwhelming sensation of having something inside my ass and a vibe on my clit. I knew that very soon I would reach my peak.

The longer I held the vibe on my clit the more I had trouble focusing on thrusting the other toy in and out so I eventually gave that up. I opted instead to just hold it as deep inside myself and focus on the feelings provided by the one on my clit and the fullness.

I came harder than I had ever thought possible within seconds of focusing on my clit only. I could feel the muscles in my ass pushing and pulling on the cock and was surprised. I had never known those muscles contracted much the same as a pussy would. I also noticed that those contractions kind of hurt when there was something inside there. That was more painful than putting it inside there, but even at that, it was still very satisfying.

When I was finished, all cleaned up and dressed, I could still feel the toy cock inside my ass and it felt wonderful to know I had done it.

I couldn't wait to tell Dave that now I would be willing to try and let him inside there. Now that I knew, I could handle it with a toy cock, I was very impatient to try it with a real one but I wasn't sure how to approach the conversation.

The next day I was sore and was very glad that I hadn't mentioned it to him as of yet. I would wait until the pain was gone, and then figure out a way to discuss that I wanted him inside there.

As luck would have it, I ended up waiting a couple months. It didn't hurt for that long, just I couldn't figure out a way to throw in "hey, want to go anal?" into conversation.

I'm still not sure how the subject came up, but it did, and it ended with me telling Dave that I wouldn't be against anal if he wanted to try it out. I did say that I wasn't sure, if I could take it or not but that I would like the chance. I left out the fact that I had gone solo on it.

Dave being the type man that he is, he didn't say, "Well let's start." or anything of that nature. It took him a couple weeks to work up to it.

We had been fooling around and there was little doubt that we were going to have sex. He was fooling around with that rear entrance ⬚uite a bit running the vibrator over it and stuff. He didn't attempt to put anything inside there at first, though by this time I really hoped that he would. I wanted him to put something inside there more every time that the vibe rubbed across the outside of it.

Dave dropped the vibrator and used his finger instead, rubbing it against my asshole. Then he began trying to push his finger inside me just a little bit. Testing my response and watching to make sure that I didn't object. I didn't. I didn't mind at all.

He did that for a little while and then stopped, and I kind of expected him to not go there because he focused his attention more on the pussy area than "back there". I resigned myself to straight sex, although admittedly I was disappointed. I had had the toy. I wanted to try it out for real now.

We continued on fooling around as always. A few kisses here and touches there, a little bit of oral sex and I was into it. I always like the fooling around, and more often than not, there doesn't seem to be enough of it. I especially found that I wanted his touches back there since he had teased around a little bit. I didn't want to push it though, even now. I wanted to wait and see if it was something that he really wanted to do.

My most favorite position is Doggy. I am a huge fan of it, and I have been since the first time I experienced it. It is better than missionary if for no other reason than hands are free to travel where ever they are needed. Dave is aware that I like it and tonight was my night because he stood up to the side of the bed and urged me to assume that position. At that point, I was ready to forget all about his teasing of the rear entrance because I knew that I would be well satisfied and still get to feel that pleasure filled pain of deep and hard penetration.

He put his cock against my pussy and pushed forward entering me with one strong sure thrust and then pulled back pulling out of me. I was getting into it quickly. I wanted to reach orgasm and didn't feel like waiting so even as he thrust himself into me I turned to look at him and asked if I could have a toy.

Dave paused and reached into the drawer by the bed and handed me my most favorite vibe for that position. The vibration is in the tip though it's a full size cock, and it works great because the length makes it easy to hang on to and keep it where I need it.

I let him resume his trusting and I pushed back against him on every in thrust in an effort to push him deeper. I was turned on enough that I felt sure if I turned on the vibe I would cum in a second. I wanted to wait though, just a little longer. I was enjoying the ride, the feel of him moving so deep inside me. As much as I wanted the orgasm, I knew that if I could wait a little longer, teasing myself with the vibe, I would cum hard.

Dave picked up the speed of his thrusts and I thought that maybe he was about to cum so I turned on the vibe and held it against myself. I knew that I was about to cum and he slowed down. The vibe felt so good to me that I couldn't slow down with him so I just held it still against me and tried to hold off my rapidly approaching orgasm.

I was keeping it at bay rather nicely, I thought, until I felt his finger rubbing against my ass hole and I felt him push it into me slightly. I cried out my orgasm and pushed myself back onto his cock in an effort to urge him to join me with his own release.

Dave just took it; he waited on me to calm down after my peak had passed before he started moving again, only it was the finger that did the moving.

I could feel him dribble a little lube down the crack of my ass as his finger moved slowly in and out, pushing a little farther in each time.

I liked the way it felt, and I started pushing back against his finger. When it would start to hurt, I would stop pushing and attempt to just rest there and let my bottom adjust. I think I had taken most of his finger, when he pulled it out and added in another finger and we began working together to get them inside me.

When I had taken most of the two fingers together, he removed them and pulled his cock from inside my pussy. I felt him pour more lube on the crack of my ass and his cock soon followed, rubbing against me and then he pointed it toward my ass hole.

Dave began pushing his cock inside and I could feel myself stretching to allow him. It did hurt, but it wasn't as painful as what I had done to myself with the vibe, so I just tried to breathe and relax.

When he popped through the outer ring and got the head of his cock inside me, I wondered if I would be able to take it after all. He was sweet though. He stopped and allowed me to adjust to that feeling.

 I wanted to get him all the way inside there, and as able pushed myself back onto him slightly.

It was turning me on to know that he was inside that hole that technically no one should be in. I reached and picked up the vibe that I had discarded once my orgasm had passed. I turned it back on and held it against myself again. As it massaged my clit for me, I relaxed and pushed myself further on to his cock.

Finally, he was all the way inside me. The vibe on my clit was working its magic and I wanted to cum again. I started pulling myself off his cock and pushing back again, rocking myself against him. The closer I got to my second peak the more I rocked.

When he took over the thrusting, I was in heaven. It was much better to have him inside me than the toy cock that I had used before. The pain was there but it felt great. I felt so full of him and regretted that we had waited so long to share that connection.

He picked up speed and I knew that this time he would cum so I focused solely on the orgasm that was about to wash over me again. I let him do what he needed to do at the speed he needed to do it. I enjoyed the feast of new things I was feeling.

Just when I thought it couldn't feel any better to have him there, I felt his cum shoot into my ass just a second before my own orgasm hit me. I could feel my ass gripping and releasing his cock and I wasn't sure how much longer I'd be able to handle it. The contractions around his cock were even more intense.

After it was over with, and Dave had pulled himself out of me, I could barely move. I was trembling from the force of my orgasms. I finally managed to move a little bit to lie down and could feel the wetness between my ass cheeks from the lube and our orgasms. He was also lying on the bed just panting, trying to get the strength needed to move and I found that rather funny.

Later, after we were both able to breathe and all cleaned up from our adventures, we discussed if it was good or not. I tried to explain to him about the pleasure/pain of it and I'm still not sure that he understood what I meant. He thanked me for letting him go there and I promised that he could go there again one day soon. What can I say? I'm hooked and it all began with a story.

UNCENSORED FUN
Anal Domination Story

The house was quiet for the first time in a long, long time. My wife had gone upstairs to get ready for bed and I took it upon myself to click the television off. I wanted to take advantage of the time and catch up on some reading. I was nose deep in War and Peace when I heard the shower shut off. For a second, I considered going up to our bedroom in an attempt to catch her naked. Then I considered the fact that I would be making an attempt to forego foreplay. It had been a long damned day, so I decided not to even make the effort. Maybe it was laziness, maybe it was fatigue, but at the end of it all, I just didn't seem to have the drive in me to make a play for impromptu sex.

My eyes were going fuzzy with the passing lines of the book, so I marked my place and closed the pages. I was burned out and I knew that I would not be able to regenerate any bit of energy without a good night of sleep. I sat the book down, stretched through an aching breath, and heaved myself out my spot. Then I trudged up the stairs to our bedroom.

The bathroom door was still closed, so I went to the guest bathroom where I kept a spare toothbrush. I scrubbed my mouth clean and returned to the bedroom.

As I breached the doorway, my eyes found their way to my wife standing next to the bed. She was wearing a light green and blue, silky, mini-length nightgown that lifted her breasts into glorious mounds. The center of her lingerie loosely hugged her waist and the skirt-like fabric at the bottom fell over her hips and the tops of her thighs. I looked further down the length of her legs and found that she was wearing her patent leather, platform heels.

She was stunning enough to have caught me in complete surprise and the energy that I thought had escaped my body suddenly returned. My cock was immediately hardening against the insides of my jeans, so I moved closer to her with every intent of taking her then and there. She moved slightly forward to meet my kiss and our tongues began dancing in and out of each other's mouths. She tasted sweet as if she had eaten a piece of candy just to give me that much more delight.

"My God, you are sexy," I said as I leaned back to look her over once more. I let my hands slide up and down her back then they slid down to her ass cheeks. In doing so, I felt the waist band of her panties and I found it peculiar that she was even wearing underwear.

She grabbed the bottom of my shirt and began to lift. I released her ass from my grip and allowed her to begin to undress me. First went my shirt. Then she undid my belt followed by my jeans. The backside of her hand rubbed my hard on as she lowered my zipper. Then, in a fluid motion, she went down to her knees as she pulled my pants down my legs. Almost immediately, she engulfed my cock with her soft and warm lips.

I felt my cock get harder in her mouth; harder than it had been in ages. It ached to become stone against the softness of her tongue and I felt a drop of pre-cum build at the tip of my member. She did not miss a beat as she sucked slowly up and back down again. All I could do was moan until I twitched.

I think she knew how close I was to cumming because she stopped her oral love making and stood in front of me. I huffed in protest, but was caught off guard by the look in her eyes. Then she smiled as she said, "I've got something for you."

Before I could question as to what she had in store, she parted her legs just enough for the front of her lingerie to spring forward.

She grabbed my right hand with her left and wrapped my fingers around her eight inch, latex cock.

"You sneaky bitch," I said playfully, but impressed by her ability to hide such a large strap on from me. The waistband of the panties I had felt was not that of a pair of panties at all. It was actually the straps of a leather harness. Then she commented, "I was afraid you felt the buckles when you rubbed my back," and she smiled again. I had not felt the buckles and I was truly surprised.

"I don't know about this baby," I said as I rubbed her cock and she rubbed mine. "It's been a long time since you've fucked me." She squeezed the middle of my shaft a little and promised that she might be gentle.

"Tell you what," I paused as her soft hand found a sensitive spot, "why don't you take this off." I tugged on her rubber dick and continued on. "I'd like to fuck you first just to make sure you get yours. Then you can fuck me and give me mine." She had no objections and was swiftly out of the harness.

I turned her back to the bed and laid her down roughly.

She fell back and the bottom of her nightgown flopped

upward. Her legs splayed open and I wasted no time. I kissed the inside of her thighs first, but did not focus too much energy on getting her hotter. I could feel the heat from her pussy and I wanted to taste her. I dove in and buried my tongue into her. I flicked her clit and licked her lips before kissing my way up her stomach. Then I kissed her breasts and moved to her neck. All the while, I plunged my right middle and ring fingers into her. She moaned as my rough hands penetrated her depths and I felt her muscles grabbing desperately at the center of my hand. I loved the feel of her pussy and proceeded to tell her about how good she felt in my hand.

"Please," was the only word she could muster between kisses and finger thrusts and "please" was the only thing I needed to hear. I placed the tip of my swollen cock at her lovely opening and I pushed into her hard and deep. She screamed out, "Holy fuck!" as I forced myself in and that made me want to fuck her even more.

A bit of compassion came over me and I allowed her a second to adjust. Her pussy muscles went into spasms, but finally relaxed. Her relaxation was my cue and I began to move my hips back and forth rhythmically.

My ass flexed with each push and I buried myself as deeply

as I could give and as deep as she could take. I started off with the intent to firmly make love to her, but I found myself fucking her harder and harder with every thrust. Before I knew it, she was hanging off the other side of the bed and I was still pounding at her insides. Moans and gasps filled the air just before she lifted her head. She reached down with both of her hands and dug her fingernails into the flesh of my ass cheeks. Her grip made me push harder into her as she began to convulse under me. I felt her hole gush with her cum and all I could do was smile.

"Ah, I needed that so bad!" she exclaimed. Then she let her grip loosen from my ass and gave me a light slap on both cheeks. "I think it's your turn."

I hesitated. "Alright, but be gentle." I begged. She answered with less assurance than I expected. "I'll be as gentle with you as you were with me."

I slid back and let myself fall out of her soaked cunt. I moved off of the bed and grabbed her hands to help her sit up. Then I stepped out her way as she stood. She grabbed the strap on from the top of the nightstand where she had left it and she proceeded to step into it.

She was still wearing her lingerie which added an extra bit of sensuality to the mix. The fact that she was wearing a strap on underneath it made it even hotter.

She fixed the buckles into place and refocused her attention back on me. I stood in front of her with my back to the bed. I leaned in for a long and passionate kiss, but I was distracted by the rubber of her cock rubbing against the skin of mine. The aura about her was intoxicating and she suddenly became more aggressive with her posture. Her hands rubbed up and down my back then over my ass as we kissed. Then she placed her hands on my chest and pushed me hard back onto the bed.

I chuckled with excitement, but was brought back to when she told me to give her my hand. I held it out to her, palm up, and she told me to get ready for her. She poured a generous amount of lube onto my hand and did the same into her hand as well.

As if posturing myself to be fucked was the most natural thing for me to do, I propped my feet up onto the edge of the bed. Then I reached down between my legs, bypassed my cock, and moved my hand to my ass.

The position I was in, knees up and feet at the edge, allowed my ass to open wide as I spread the juice over my hole. I placed the tip of my middle finger at my opening and I pushed inward. My ass resisted my very touch because it had been so long since we had played in such a fashion.

"Um, I think this is going to hurt," I said as I felt my asshole clenching against my fingers. My pulse thumped against my digit and I waited to relax a little before moving in and out of myself. I took a deep breath in and exhaled completely in hopes of relaxing a bit more. It worked and I let my ring finger glide in next to the middle. My ass clenched again and I went through the process once more.

As I fingered myself, getting ready to be fucked, I looked down to my wife. She had since wrapped her fist around her hard on and was jerking off while watching me play with my ass. "Do you like what you see," I asked with a coy tone and she nodded. "Then come and get it."

She did not have to be enticed further. She instructed me to slide further onto the bed and lift my legs. I did so and she was Quickly in between my open thighs.

I felt the tip of her monstrous phallus at the center of my hole. Then she pushed forward. I gasped as she force the head into me. "Gentle!" I pleaded and she was gracious enough to give pause. She waited only a second longer. My asshole was still twitching at the invasion when she pushed the full length of her shaft into me. "Ah!" I yelled out as the front of her hips met the mounds of my ass. Buried into me completely, she hooked her arms under my knees and lifted my legs higher. This gave her more access to my hole and she pushed in even deeper. Pain seared through my body before the absolutely full delight of being penetrated kicked in.

"Fuck me," I moaned. She complied with the re□uest. My legs were still bent at the knee and draped over her arms as she began to rock back and forth with her hips. The dildo slid out of me nearly to the tip and impaled me once more as she returned. She started slow at first, but built into a hard and swift pace that continually knocked the wind from me with each of her thrusts.

Her breasts hovered just above my stomach when she leaned over me. She was in full force as she pounded my ass. Then, just to show me she was completely in charge, she raised back upward.

She grabbed my ankles to lift my feet high above her shoulders, and she pounded harder and deeper. "Do you like the way I fuck your ass, bitch?" The words slithered out of her mouth the way you hear in a porn flick. It made pre-cum bead on the tip of my cock. I watched it drip from the head as my hard on bounced around at each slap of her hips against my ass.

"May I cum?" I begged as if I had any control over when my cock was to explode. "No," she heaved into me. I felt my face go red with anticipation. I could barely breathe. I wanted so bad to jerk off into relief. My wife apparently was having too much fun fucking my ass. "Please?" I begged once more.

"Cum for me," she commanded. I licked a wad of saliva into my hand and moved it to my cock. "Oh fuck, I'm so hard," I was amazed at how hard I actually was. I loved the feeling of a rubber cock in my ass while I stroked my member in the same rhythm of her poundings.

She fucked me faster and I rubbed faster until I began to spurt. The first hot stream hit the bottom of my chin and fell across my neck. The ensuing blasts covered my chest and stomach until my orgasm subsided.

My wife pushed one last hard pump deep into me to make sure that every last drop had come about. She was successful in milking me dry, so she slowly extracted her cock from me. Once she was out of me, I felt just how stretched my ass was from her ruthless fucking. I felt abused in a way that I had not felt in a long time and it made my cock twitch one last creamy bit.

My front was coated with cum and my asshole was slathered with lube. I was a mess of ecstasy and all I could think to say was, "I love you."

We cleaned up and went to bed just to get some of that much needed rest.

HAZING DESIRES

Voyeurism Embarrassed Story

Leslie stood in the corner with a wine cooler in her hand and looked over the guys at the party. A lot of cute guys. All thin and wiry track athletes-which was a turn on for her-with their cut cheeks and tan faces and sharp shoulders and elbows. But she was shy and didn't exactly know how to work the room. She watched two of her new running friends chatting eagerly with the faster male runners, upperclassmen-one she knew by name from his wins last season. Even though she was new to the school this week, she had followed the team's social feeds since she was accepted in the spring.

"Hi," a pleasant male voice surprised her, with a bit of slur. "Are you new to the team?"

She turned to look at a particularly thin and wiry track athlete-a handsome young devil-who had snuck up beside her. He had a goofy grin on his face to which she couldn't help but smile in response. She put out her hand.

"Leslie. Yes, I am a frosh." She motioned to the partygoers in front of them. "To be honest, it's all a little overwhelming." It wasn't clear whether she meant this party, leaving home that week to be a freshman in college, or joining the running team.

"Brian," he said, taking her hand, the goofy smile only

increasing. "Welcome to the team. I've had a few drinks, so excuse my boldness," he said, waving the margarita in his hand in a wide circle to illustrate, his unsteady motion only confirming his statement, "but you are very pretty."

Leslie blushed and ran her hand through her long bangs. "Brian, thank you, but I think you've had too many tonight. Let me guess, you don't drink regularly?"

"No ma'am. I keep it clean all season for the team."

She laughed. "Yes, me too. But it does mean that your-what, 120 pounds?-can't handle very much alcohol. I think your liver gave up the fight already."

"No, I'm fine! I'm only on my third drink, or maybe fourth." He held his fingers out to illustrate, but they didn't cooperate in showing the number he wanted so he looked more closely at his hand and tried again. Leslie laughed. He was a lightweight.

"Brian, listen my boy, you are done for tonight. We've got the first workout tomorrow and you will be in bad shape if you drink any more." Leslie looked around to see where she could find a refuge to sober him up with a few glasses of water. She put her arm around his shoulders to steady him.

"Let's go out to the patio."

They sat a while in the warm fall evening air and talked about their lives at college, what it was like to go from high school to a college athletic team. They both were standouts in their local districts, but apprehensive of the work it might take to be a contributing part at the college level, even though the team was only NCAA division II. Like many high school athletes, they were grappling with what athletics meant to their lives and how much they wanted it to define them.

The evening ended with Leslie finding one of Brian's roommates to guide him home. While he went to fetch their jackets from the closet, she leaned into Brian and gave him a kiss on the lips. His eyes opened wide and when he realized what was happening he focused on her face and tried to kiss her back. It wasn't the best kiss ever, but he hit mostly lips and a tingle went down her spine. Maybe college wasn't going to be so bad after all, she thought.

The week was as tough as they feared. It was what they called, not surprisingly, "hell week" for the incoming freshmen of both genders. Five solid days of workouts trying to keep up with the upperclassmen who had already been running for at least two years more than them, with stronger and more mature bodies. It was the week before classes started, at least, so they had no other academic duties to contend with. The schedule was all-consuming: ⬚uick breakfast, run in the morning, stretching, lunch with the team, some light work in the weight room in the afternoon, then an evening run followed by dinner and an early bedtime. It gave Leslie and Brian both a feeling for what it would be like to be a professional athlete.

The two found only one occasion during the week when they could meet privately, one night in an alley behind the pizza joint. Neither had a dorm room to themselves, so they understood that all they could expect would be kissing and a little touching in a clandestine public place. Brian leaned against Leslie on the alley wall, traced his finger against her blonde hairline from her forehead down to her chin, and gave her a gentle kiss. She melted. His hand reached to her and gently pressed against her small breast.

Leslie's figure, like that of all the girls on the team, was slender. She had some curves, but they were subtle. Brian's fingers had no trouble finding those curves, though, as well as the hard point of Leslie's little nipple that he could feel through her shirt. He played his index finger slowly back and forth over it while he kissed her, and then pinched firmly while he leaned in for a deeper kiss. She sucked in her breath as a little spasm ran up and down her whole body.

They both knew the last day of hell week was going to be hard. Before the afternoon-and final-workout session, organized by the upperclassmen, there was a lot of fuss made about it. A lot of shouting and encouraging, like, "You've got 90 minutes more to make it on the team, hang in there, you can get through it!" Technically, everybody had already secured a spot on the team based on their high school times, so there wasn't any serious stress about being cut, but as a rule athletes have a very competitive personality type and every new freshman guy and girl wanted to put in their best.

They ran repeatedly up and down the hill behind the campus that featured a number of criss-crossing dirt trails. "The Hill" was simply what everybody called it, and it would have been a pretty venue for a relaxing stroll if it weren't a place where so much pain was inflicted on these college athletes' muscles and minds in their intense training sessions. The runners went elsewhere for their recreation in the off-season part of the school year.

"One last rep now, girls. Ready. Go!" a senior girl with a whistle and clipboard shouted, clicking her watch as the freshman girls launched up the left side trail. The boys had left an hour earlier to run their own hell week drills on the upper part of The Hill. A final hard sprint down the shallow slopes left the girls gasping, with only a few more minutes to go for their hell week. Some girls flopped down on the grass breathing hard. They hadn't been so exhausted, maybe ever, in their training, all of them working so hard to impress their new college teammates.

"Line up, you only have five minutes left. You aren't done yet. Now!" The senior girl with the whistle blew it loudly over the clearing to scare the freshmen into a line, where they were positioned so that with their hands on heads they just touched elbows with the girl next to them.

They went through a few coordinated stretching exercises, after which the senior blew her whistle and yelled, "Any girl wearing a shirt, take it off and put it at your feet." The girls were standing in a line in the grass at the edge of the merging of two wide dirt trails coming down off the hill. About half of them had stripped to sports bras already, but the ones wearing shirts, after a confused look left and right, responded to the urgency of the whistle and pulled them over their heads and dropped them on the grass by their feet.

"Looking good, team, hold still now and look straight ahead," the senior said, walking down the line and staring at each face like a sergeant in one of those Navy SEAL training movies. There were fourteen new girls to the team this year, a large incoming class, and a very attractive group on the whole. The girls had their hair pinned up, faces shining with radiant skin, eyes blazing from their exertions, and their small, fit chests were still heaving in and out from their final sprint just moments ago. "These are the bodies we have to work with for this year. You will work hard, and we will mold you, shape you into winning athletes!"

She stopped at the head of the line and looked at her watch, then glanced up The Hill. "Only one minute to go now, and you will be on the team. You've worked hard all week, this is your final test. When I blow the whistle, you will pull off your bras and put your hands on your heads. Elbows should touch your neighbor."

She paused to let it sink in. There was total silence on the line. Every girl was thinking to herself something like: What the fuck? Take off my bra, to make the team? Are the other girls going to do this? We've worked so hard all week, should we just do this and get it over with? The clearing was empty of people, the birds were chirping, and the sun was shining. Some thought, it was a beautiful, peaceful setting and a lovely fall day, so it wouldn't be the worst thing to go for a little topless nudity on a dare.

But regardless of the internal conversation in each girl's head, when the senior blared on the whistle and screamed in their faces, "Bras off! Now!" each one immediately jumped into action, scrambling to pull off the sports bra and throw her hands in the air, elbows out to her neighbor. They made a beautiful line of tan and fit flesh.

After Leslie slipped off her bra and tossed it to her feet, she put her elbows up behind her head and stuck out her chest like the other girls. She had put so much effort into that last workout to keep up that it wasn't like she didn't care that she was topless-she was a shy girl, afterall-but she was so relieved to be done running for the day that the nudity washed over her. When you've pushed your mind and body that hard, other stresses fade into the background. In fact, that's why she got into running in the first place, it put everything else in life into perspective.

Leslie was at the head of the line, so after the senior went past her to the next girl in her inspection, she looked down to her own breasts and was pleased: the familiar gentle curves of white flesh highlighted by her small, hard and dark nipples. A glance down the line showed her the neat row of girls all standing at attention at the edge of the trail. She had seen plenty of nudity in shower rooms, but nothing so curious as this scene.

From the grass where their running shoes rested, she remarked on each pair of athletic tanned calves and thighs, a colorful pair of shorts-mostly pink or light blue colors-toned and tanned muscular stomachs still pulsing in and out from the exertion of the workout- and possibly the nervousness of this hazing-then up to the curves of fourteen pairs of beautiful, small breasts, highlighted by the uniform and seemingly endless row of pert nipples on display: just one cute little bump after another, down the whole line. Some tits jiggled with the girls' nerves, as they couldn't hold perfectly still in that position. All of the runners were slender, with tight and firm breasts resting high on their chests. There might have been two B-cup girls in the whole line, if that.

The senior girl barked out, "Very nice girls. You've got one minute to hold out those little titties!"

The girls waited with their minds blank, just trying to endure this until the end, and hoping it would come soon. "40 seconds!" the senior shouted. Then they heard the sounds. One by one the girls realized what the sounds were, and eyes flew open and their hearts □uickened.

"You don't move a muscle!" the senior shouted. "30 seconds to go!"

From around the corner they came. The entire boys team, about forty of them. They were jogging single- file, not racing, and they were on course directly down from The Hill and across the clearing to run right past the row of topless girls thrusting their nipples out to the trail.

"You hold and look straight ahead!" the senior girl shouted to the freshman, some of whose faces were starting to crack with nervous tension. More than a few muttered under their breaths, but none of them moved. Nobody had the courage to break ranks, and the senior girl was right in front of them, watching intently to call out and punish any movement. Their small breasts stuck out prominently to the trail, the beautiful soft tissue of fourteen girls' nipples on display.

The first boys met the line of girls and slowed while they looked at the topless figures. The boys' faces went into a sort of shock, it was too much nudity to take in at once and appreciate, although they tried, scanning up and down from face to breasts again and again for each girl as they passed. Their brains worked furiously as they tried to commit to memory the shape and size and color of each girl's nude chest. The boys in the middle and back of the line kept coming so the ones in front couldn't slow down as they would have liked to, but got pushed past the girls in a hurry.

"10 seconds to go!" the senior girl shouted.

Leslie's was on the far end of the line, the last part the boys ran past, and even though she was supposed to be looking straight ahead, she was searching out of the corner of her eye for Brian. Her tits were on display to all the guys like every other girls' was, but she focused on getting through this by thinking she was showing them to Brian alone. There he was, finally, at the back of the line. He ran past and winked at her just as the senior blew the whistle. He didn't make a secret of his gaze dropping from her face to her breasts, and he raised his eyebrows and smiled his approval as he turned to look back at her while jogging away. Leslie covered herself up and couldn't resist a small smile at his tribute.

"Done! Good job, girls. Welcome to the team!" the senior yelled, as the girls all scrambled to put on their tops again. Their faces were as red as when they had finished the last hill workout.

Later that night, after a few beers, Leslie held her head against Brian's shoulder at the end-of-hell-week party. She shook her head, remembering that afternoon as she would the rest of her life. "I can't believe all you guys ran past us and saw all our tits. Oh my God, I heard about hazing in college, but I never thought I would be in one. And agree to do it."

"What do you mean all the girls? I saw only one girl in that blur of naked bodies. A very pretty girl." He smiled at her. "But come on, it wasn't all bad was it? Wasn't it was a little bit fun? Didn't it make your heart race, seeing the whole gang of us come around the corner while you were holding your hands up, tits out, knowing that we were about to run right past you, and you couldn't cover up?"

Leslie punched him, even though there might have been a small kernel of truth in what he said. "Yeah, your fantasy, I know. You guys will be jerking off to that for years. I hope there's some way you guys pay us back!"

"Well, I don't know exactly what, but there's supposed to be this thing next weekend at the retreat. I don't think it will be the like what you girls did today, but a couple of the guys told us to get ready to show our stuff. I think you'll get your payback."

"Oh, I'm going to be getting my payback all right." She looked down at his wiry figure and ran her finger from his big runner's chest to his narrow waist and then to the bulge on his shorts, brushing against that bulge and feeling its shape through the fabric. Then she raised her head and glanced around at the house to see if there were any bedrooms to sneak off to. "In fact, I'm pretty sure I'm going to get my payback in just a few minutes."

I would like to invite you to read another one of
my books that I think you will really enjoy.
The book is called:

**_" BDSM DARK SEX:8 Unraveled Explicit
Stories For Adults VOL.2"_**

Enjoy!

PLAYFUL WEATHER

Outdoor Voyeur/Exhibitionism Story

All through high school and most of college, I never felt good about my body. Objectively I knew it was fine—a little flabby at worst—but I could never shake the insecurities of the chubby kid I had been before puberty evened out my baby fat. Junior year, I decided to do something about it. I started copying the exercise and diet regime of my track star roommate, Alice, and by the end of the year I was falling in love with myself, how toned and strong I had become.

That's when I started wanting to show off. I threw out my baggy running shorts and got a pair of tiny spandex ones like Alice wore. At the gym I wore them with only a sports bra, so that everyone could see my newly flat tummy. After a lifetime of hiding my body, it felt good to see the guys turn their heads as they walked by me on the treadmill.

My new confidence didn't yet extend outside of the gym, though, so on the way there and back I covered up with an oversized t-shirt. The shirt hid my shorts completely, and Alice teased that it looked like I had nothing on underneath. I blushed, secretly as excited as I was embarrassed. Did I actually like the idea that someone might think I was half-dressed in public?

I worked out early most mornings, and occasionally the

locker room was completely empty when I got done. I liked the opportunity that gave me to check myself out in the full-length mirrors. I might spend upwards of ten minutes flexing my biceps or looking over my shoulder to admire how firm my butt had gotten. One morning, when the gym was especially empty, I decided I wanted to see how my body looked without the sports bra flattening my breasts. Even without it they were small, but seeing their softness unrestrained changed what I was feeling. Pride in my fitness shifted toward something more sensual. I took a quick glance around, saw no sign of anyone, and pulled off my shorts as well.

Now instead of posing like a bodybuilder, I started posing more like a playmate. I pushed my breasts together and tweaked my nipples to make them hard. I turned around and squeezed my ass, then bent forward until I could see the hairless lips of my pussy. Just as I slid my finger between them, I heard the locker room door open. In a panic I rushed back to my locker without picking up my clothes. Luckily I had my t-shirt, which I pulled on before I went back to pick up my workout gear.

I caught a glimpse of myself in the mirror and saw that I was completely covered by the t-shirt. The shape of my breasts was slightly more apparent without the sports bra, but other than that putting the rest of my clothes back on wouldn't change the way I looked at all. So why bother? I thought. It wasn't far back to my dorm room. If the flush already filling my body didn't give me away, no one would be the wiser. I dropped the shorts and bra in my backpack, pulled it on, and walked out of the locker room.

My first step out of the locker room was amazing, but the real thrill came when I got outside. A storm seemed to be moving in, and almost as soon as I set foot on the sidewalk a gust of wind traveled all the way up my body. It made my nipples go rock hard, and I was sure they'd be visible through the t-shirt. That thought made my pussy burn, and I could tell that I was blushing even more than before. I picked up my pace, as much out of desperation to get to my room and touch myself as out of fear of being seen. I was half way up the stairs to my dorm when I heard a man's voice calling my name.

It was John—tall, blue-eyed John, the guy I'd had a hopeless crush on for the past two-and-a-half years. The guy who barely spoke to me while I lingered just outside his conversations at parties. The guy who, if I'm being honest, had motivated me to get in shape. The guy who was flagging me down on the street, now, when I was half-naked and dripping wet and wanted nothing except to rip off the one piece of clothing I had on and cram my vibrator up my pussy as fast as I could.

"Hey, you doing anything right now?" he said. "You want to go grab breakfast or something?"

"Sure! Just let me run up stairs and change. I just got back from the gym." That's what I should've said. It's what one-year-ago, unconfident me would've said, if she had ever been in this situation in the first place. What I actually said, as I turned back down the stairs with the wind still whipping across my bare pussy: "Yeah, I'm starved."

What can I say? I had wanted to be naked with him since freshman year, and if this was as close as I might ever get, I was going to make it last.

We started off towards the dining hall, cutting through a little park at the center of campus. Our talk was awkward—we really didn't know each other that well, and I was in no frame of mind to be witty. He kept clumsily shifting his pace to drop back a step or two behind me, or pausing to admire flowers that were already wilted. At different points he stopped to tie each of his shoes, which didn't seem to be untied. When he made a show of somehow dropping his keys from inside his shorts pocket, I was dead certain: he knew.

But how? I reach back to feel my t-shirt behind me and, to my horror, felt nothing but bare skin. I found the hem of the shirt bunched up beneath my backpack and tugged it down. "Oh shit," I said. I was ready to run at full speed back to my room, but instead, I black out for a second, just long enough to land in John's arms.

He led me to a bench and sat beside me. "Are you okay?"

I still wanted to run, but I was too unsteady. "How much did you see?" I asked, my voice quavering. I was afraid I might cry.

"Was... was that not on purpose?" he answered. "Oh man, I would never have..."

"No! I mean... kind of? But no one was supposed to know."

Now he was blushing too. "Well, don't worry, I won't tell anybody. Just breathe, ok? It's alright."

His concern was sweet, and it calmed me down immediately. Suddenly I felt safer than I had since I was by myself in the locker room. But he was still curious, too. The second he was sure I wasn't going to pass out, he asked, "Do you have anything on at all under there?"

I shook my head. "Maybe I should go back to my room and change, huh?" I said. "Will you come with me, and tell me if it starts to ride up again?"

He agreed and we started back, but we had only gone a few steps when he nudged me to pull my shirt down. A few steps further and another nudge. "Maybe I should just take your backpack," he offered.

Looking up at him with my tiny purple backpack slung over one shoulder, I felt grateful that it was John out of everyone on campus who had caught me trotting up my dorm stairs with my ass out. I was just about to thank him when the sky opened up, and we were both instantly drenched. This was a bigger problem for me, since I was wearing nothing but a white t-shirt.

John pointed out a magnolia tree, and we hid in the cave created by its branches, where only a few drops of rain made it through. Under the overcast sky it was twilight inside. Even if anyone had been out in the rain, I doubted they could have seen us. The tree was like a private cocoon within the larger cocoon of the storm. I looked over at John and found his eyes on the t-shirt that clung to my body.

"I have some other clothes in the backpack," I said. "Could you hand it to me and turn around?"

He did, and I dragged the soaking t-shirt over my head. I found myself just standing there, staring at his back, gym shorts in hand, stark naked. I didn't want to get dressed. I didn't want him to keep his back turned. I wanted him to see me, all of me. I let the shorts fall and pressed myself against his back, wrapping my arms around his thick chest.

"You really saved me, you know," I said. "I'd like to show my appreciation."

Instantly he turned and I was smothered by his mouth, his hands. He lifted me up against the tree trunk as I wrapped my legs around him. I could feel his erection through his shorts, thrusting against my bare pussy. I pushed him back, only so that I could drop to my knees in front of him and pull down his shorts. His cock sprung out, as large as it had been all the dozens of times I fantasized this moment, and I wrapped my lips around it. I took it as far into my mouth as I could and still had room to stroke it with both hands.

He let me suck him for a long, blissful moment before he pulled my head away by my wet hair.

Then he pushed me down on my back in the dirt and climbed astride my chest, pressing his cock back into my mouth as he reached behind to finger my pussy. The second he touched my clit I bucked, angling my body so that his fingers slipped inside me.

"You want it, don't you?" he growled. I let his cock go from my mouth so that I could beg for it in my pussy.

He didn't make me beg for long. He rolled me face down, pulled my ass into the air, and fucked me like a wild animal beneath that tree. My cheek was ground into the damp black soil with every thrust. My hands gathered little piles of roots and weeds as my body began to quiver, then shake uncontrollably against his steady force. It was only after I came, as loudly as I ever have, that I remembered where we were. A quick look around suggested we were safe.

My climax didn't slow him down any—he was still pounding me into the ground like a machine driving a post. He was slumped across my back, his mouth at my ear. Now it was his turn to beg. "I love your ass," he panted. "Please let me come on your ass." Unable to speak, I nodded as best as I could.

He pulled out and, with only a few strokes, came not just on my ass but far up my back, into my hair. He collapsed against the tree trunk, and I rolled on my side to look at him. Now that he and I were silent, I could hear that the rain had quieted too. It had almost stopped. A cool breeze found its way into our hideout and set off tremors in my still tingling skin.

"We'd better not hang out too long, huh?" he said, still catching his breath.

"No," I answered. "We'd better get back as fast as we possibly can."

I stood in front of him for a moment and let him take in the full length of my body—glistening with rain, smeared with mud, flushed with fading heat. Then I grabbed my backpack and, leaving the t-shirt behind, sprinted out across the grass.

DREAM LOVE
Beach Nudist Story

The campfire embers gradually faded from white and reddish-orange to gray and black. As the campfire died, the darkness from the surrounding woods edged closer eventually enveloping me. I'd been sitting for a couple of hours staring into the fire and poking it now and then with a long stick to keep it burning. I'd been thinking about the evening ahead and how much fun I was going to have doing something I'd never done before. Now it was dark enough to get started. I got up and took off my shirt. Then I cast my shorts aside and stood there in the darkness as the occasional flames flickered and briefly lit my naked body.

I wasn't the greatest male specimen on two feet. I knew that, but for a dude approaching the epochal age of 30, I was in reasonable shape. I should be. I'd ridden my bike over 2000 miles that summer and kayaked a few hundred more. But, now I was about to do something I had always wanted to do but had never had the opportunity or guts to try: ride my bike totally nude (well, except for my sandals).

I got on my bike and headed down the trail. As my eyes adjusted to the dark, I could see the trail as a gray path amongst the dark shadows ahead of me. The grass and bushes on either side were dark by comparison. I pedaled slowly and uneasily at first. I'd walked the trail that afternoon, so I pretty much knew what was ahead, but, even though it was late (almost midnight), I still feared I would meet someone on the trail. It added to the thrill and I felt a tingling in my groin as my balls rocked from side to side with each turn of the pedals. Needless to say, I had a respectable hard-on.

My mind formulated a plan: in the unlikely event that I did meet someone, so what? If anyone were out on the trail, I'd just grunt a greeting and ride on as if everything were □uite normal. What could be so wrong with a midnight ride even if the rider wore no clothes? Besides, I reasoned, there weren't many campers in the campground, and, aside from the young lady in the trailer across from mine, most were elderly and had probably gone to bed long ago.

The young lady's name, I'd learned, was Beth and she too liked to bike and had brought her bike with her.

We'd talked briefly and I'd made a mental note to ask her to go biking with me before we left. However, I didn't want to appear too forward, so I'd decided to wait until she got settled and we got to know each other a little better.

I pedaled on. A mile down the trail I came to the road that led down to the lake and the beach. I knew from my earlier investigation that there was a gate on the road and that it was locked at 9:00 pm and remained locked until 6:00 am. So, in theory, I would have the beach and the road to myself until 6:00 tomorrow morning.

The road made a loop down to the beach and on past it to the picnic area then back around to connect with itself near where the trail came in.

I pedaled around the loop slowly and cautiously the first time. Then I pedaled out to the gate to make sure it was locked. It was. I pedaled back to the beach. It was a warm night. The sun had been down for several hours but it was still in the 80s. I pedaled around the loop again. I had broken into a good sweat and decided it was time for a swim.

I left my bike leaning on a picnic table and walked out into the water. I stood there with the water just over my cock and balls, enjoying the coolness of it and listening to the sound of the waves lapping against the shore.

A full moon had risen over the lake. It was marvelous to see the huge orange disk coming up over the mountains beyond the far shore of the lake. A full moon on the Summer Solstice, that could only mean good things were instore. I loved nature and when nature put on a show, I paid attention.

Finally, breaking my reverie, I dove and swam to the rope boundary of the swimming area. The cool water felt good on my bare skin. I loved swimming nude. No clothes restricting my movements, my cock and balls swaying gently in the water, what could be better? I swam over to the marker buoy on one corner of the swimming area, then to the other corner and back. I felt totally free and uninhibited. The only thing missing was a companion to share this wonderful experience.

I'd always hoped to find someone who thought the way I did and liked to do the same weird stuff that I loved to do like biking and swimming nude.

I swam some more and was thinking about getting out when I heard a noise. It sounded like a bike coming down the road. I listened intently. Someone was definitely coming. The sound of tires crunching on the gravel road grew louder. Keep cool, I thought. Don't panic. Besides, there was nothing much I could do. I swam to one of the buoys. At least behind it I wouldn't be quite so obvious. The moon was behind me and almost as bright as a street light. My heart pounded in my ears as I held my breath trying to pick up every sound.

As I watched, I saw a petite figure ride up on a bicycle. She leaned it against the picnic table next to mine.

"Hey there, you alone?" A beautiful female voice called out.

It was Beth, the young lady I had met that afternoon. I was so amazed I was practically speechless.

"Just me enjoying a late night swim." I replied.

"Mind if I join you?" Beth was standing on the beach now.

"Sure, be my guest," I finally managed to blurt out. "The water's great."

I watched as she shed her shorts and tank top. To my amazement, she was not wearing anything underneath. My cock stiffened as I pondered the potential of this new development. She walked back to the picnic table and tossed her clothes on it. There was enough moonlight that I could clearly see the twitch in her cute little ass as she walked. My cock got even harder.

"How'd you know it was me? How'd you know I was here?" I asked.

"I was watching when you left camp. Sorry, I guess I'm a bit of a peeping Tom. I've been watching you all night. When I saw you ride off naked, I decided to follow and see what you were up to. I figured you might be meeting someone."

"Do you do this often?" I teased, "I mean, follow nude men on bicycles?"

"No, this is my first time. I'm usually very cautious around strangers. But I sensed you were safe. You have an interesting aura about you that made me curious. I wanted to get to know you better, but I didn't want you to think I was one of those 'easy' girls. How about you? Do you go for nude bicycle rides often?"

"No, actually this is my first one. I've always wanted to but could never work up the courage or find the right place for one."

I watched as she waded out into the water. Beth was a beautiful, petite blonde and I remembered from our brief encounter earlier that she had a great sense of humor and a very disarming smile. I had liked her immediately and now

I liked her even more. A girl who wore no underwear, rode her bike at night and followed a naked guy to the beach was definitely someone I wanted to know better. I had the feeling we would become good friends, and maybe even more than friends. I discretely played with my stiff cock and stroked it a couple of times. Yes, I definitely wanted to get close to this girl. The fact that she was here told me she felt the same way.

Beth waded in waist deep then quickly dove into the water. "I didn't bring a swimming suit," she said as she swam out into deeper water.

"Yeah, I noticed." I said. "Guess you know I didn't either."

"Swimming suits are definitely over-rated," I ventured. It was lame, but I couldn't think of anything else to say under the circumstances. This was new territory for me and I surely did not want to scare Beth away or give her any cause for concern.

"I'm glad you decided to do this. It was really hot and sticky in the camp tonight and I wanted to go for a swim, but I didn't want to go alone. I thought of asking you, but then I didn't have a suit and I wasn't sure how you would react.

Then, I saw you pedal off in the buff, I figured I'd just follow along and see what you were up to."

I had my arms stretched out to either side and draped over the boundary rope which rested under my armpits. Beth swam over to where I was then disappeared underwater.

I felt her lips kiss the tip of my dick before she rose up out of the water, wiping her hands back over her face and to get the water out of her eyes and smoothing her hair back behind her head in one easy stroke.

"Just inspecting the merchandise," she laughed, "Hope you don't mind." I felt her foot massaging my balls as she spoke. Finally, she gave my balls a soft, playful kick.

"Hope it met with your approval," I grinned.

"Well, let's just say I liked what I saw even though it was hard to get a good look with water in my eyes." Beth laughed again and gave me a playful push. Then swam a short distance away.

"Truthfully, " I admitted, "I really wanted to invite you to come for a midnight ride and go skinny dipping with me, but

I was afraid you would think I was a weirdo and wouldn't want to have anything to do with me. I liked you from the moment I first saw you and wanted to get to know you better. Last thing I wanted to do was scare you away."

"Come here," Beth said. "Let's get better acquainted."

I swam closer. She reached out her hand. I took it and she pulled me close to her. We hugged. Her breasts felt good against mine and my boner was clamped between her pubic mound and mine.

"Oh, you are all primed and ready to go!" She exclaimed. "That's good because I've been so horny all day I was thinking I was going to have to do myself tonight. But then I met you and I thought, 'Maybe'. You have a nice smile and I noticed a bulge in your shorts when we were talking earlier. I figured a camper, a fellow biker and someone who likes to kayak couldn't be all bad. Then you took off on your bike totally naked and I just had to follow."

"Do you often follow naked men on bicycles?" I teased

"No, you are my first." She smiled. Then, dove and I felt her warm lips on the cool head of my cock. She kissed it several times and blew bubbles at it, then surfaced, laughing.

"I've always wanted to do that." She said, a gleeful smile on her face.

I pinched myself right there in front of her. "Just have to make sure I am not dreaming," I said. "I've always dreamed of this happening, but never thought it actually would."

"Am I your dream girl?" She teased. "You are that and more," I said.

With that she dove again and this time I felt her mouth envelope my cock which now was rock hard. I was glad the lake was spring fed and the water was clear and clean.

Beth came up gasping for breath. She grabbed my hand. "Come with me, bad boy," she said as she pulled me toward shore.

 "I have a blanket and towel in the basket on my trike. I also brought a six-pack of cold beer in case you're thirsty."

"Now I know I've died and gone to heaven," I said as I followed her to shore.

We found a grassy spot and spread the blanket. After drying each other off, we sat down and popped the top on a couple of cold ones.

Beth took a swig of hers and smiled, "Tell me, how come you rode down here naked

"It is something I've always wanted to do. I scoped out the place earlier today and figured I'd have the path and beach to myself. The remote possibility that I might meet someone along the way made it exciting."

"Well, you did meet someone, didn't you?" Beth smiled.

"Yes, I did, and I'm very glad I did. But, I never expected to meet someone like you. I was worried about running into some prude who wouldn't take kindly to a nude male biker or swimmer, even at this hour.

But, I have to admit, the possibility that someone might catch me and be offended actually excited me. However, I'm ecstatic that you caught me and were not offended."

"Nudity has never bother me," Beth admitted. "I like being naked and I don't mind other people being naked around me as long as they behave themselves. Just because a woman is naked does not mean she wants to have sex with any man that comes along. Some guys don't get that. For me, naked is just another way of dressing. If it is hot out or I'm going swimming, I'd prefer not to wear anything."

"I feel the same way. I guess I'm a bit of an exhibitionist, but I've always been afraid of getting caught. To tell the truth, I just like doing ordinary things nude. I wish I could go nude all the time.

Clothing should always be optional. I wish people would get over it. I know some nudists misbehave and do things like jacking off in public that offend others, but most don't. Don't get me wrong, I don't think there is anything wrong with having sex in public on a nudist beach. If people want to do that or give a blowjob or whatever, I'm fine with that.

But if some guy starts staring or making unwanted advances; that is something else."

"Speaking of sex on a beach," Beth smiled and eyed my now drooping cock. "You seem to have lost your focus. Let me help you with that."

She reached over and began stroking my cock back to life. It didn't take long. I lay back on my elbows and Beth knelt down and began kissing and sucking on the head of my cock. She teased my pee hole with her tongue then licked up and down my shaft. All the while, she gently played with my balls, caressing and gently s□ueezing them between her thumb and forefinger.

"Ouch!" I protested when she s□ueezed a little too hard. "It hurts when you s□ueeze so hard."

"Sorry," She said. "I don't have much experience with men's balls. I didn't realize they were so sensitive."

Once I was good and hard, she put her mouth where her hand had been. Her head bobbed up and down on my shaft. Each time she went down a little farther.

She gagged a little at first, but kept at it. Finally, she was taking the full length. It felt wonderful and I could feel the ecstasy building in my loins. I arched my hips to meet her and tried to thrust even deeper. That didn't seem to bother her. She had her eyes closed and was lost to the world around us.

I let her work me up to a near boil, but I wanted to be sure she was satisfied, too. So, before I came, I somehow summoned the strength to tap her on the shoulder. "My turn," I hissed between clenched teeth. A few more strokes and it would be all over. Then I'd need at least a few hours to recharge. With other women, I might have let them continue and blown my wad into their mouth, but I felt different about Beth. I wanted to make sure she was having as good a time as I was. I wasn't sure how much she enjoyed sucking on my cock, but she sure seemed more than okay with it.

She reluctantly let my cock slip from her puckered lips and lay back on the blanket as I knelt over her and began kissing and nibbling at the little nobs on her pert B-cup tits. The nipples were nice and hard and she moaned when I gently bit each one. I continued to play with them between my fingers as I straddled her and kissed my way down to her pubic mound.

She had a cute little triangle of curly blonde hair that pointed the way to my destination. I kissed her there and continued south, kissing one side and then the other of her lower lips. Finally, I found her dripping love spot with my tongue and nuzzled her clit with my nose. I knew my scruffy beard would leave a rash on her inner thighs, but she didn't seem to mind. She spread her knees wide to give me full access. After a while she was rotating her hips and thrusting her pelvis up into my face. I knew she was getting close. I brought her to the edge, then backed off.

Rising to my knees and positioning myself between her legs, I lay forward and with her help, my cock found its target and inched its way in. She held me tight for a moment while her pussy adjusted to my hard cock. It was sizeable, too, if I do say so myself. A good 7" long and 1-1/2 inches thick. Good enough to probe the depths of any pussy. I gave Beth the full 7" and she rose to meet it. I pulled out until just the head remained. Her moist lips caressed my cockhead and beckoned me to plunge back in. I thrust again fast and deep as she rotated her hips and rose to meet me. Then I was pulling out and plunging deep again and again and again. Faster. Deeper.

Our world dissolved. There was nothing but my cock head and her pussy with us panting and grunting in the background. The pressure mounted and finally I could hold it no longer and blew my wad deep inside her. I could feel spurt after spurt of warm white liquid cum shooting into her. With each spurt, I felt her pussy muscles contract, squeezing every last drop out of me. I lost track at 10 spurts, but I think there could have been 12. Ten was my record and was easily an eighth cup of the best cum ever shot from a dick. I was glad I had saved myself the past two weeks. Giving Beth my full load sent her over the edge, too.

"Milk me good," I whispered.

With one final spurt, I sent the last of my load into her. I'd never had such good sex and I was sure I'd shot more of a load than ever before. I collapsed on her and lay there panting for several seconds. I could feel her pussy contractions milking every drop of cum from my spent cock.

I started to pull out, but Beth held me tight. "No, stay. Stay still until it goes limp," She insisted.

We lay still for several minutes. Finally, I heard her sweet voice.

"That was wonderful," she purred, "Simply wonderful. I've never come like that before. Where have you been all my life?"

"It was good for me, too," I said. But, as I said it, I knew it was one of the biggest understatements I'd ever made.

"You are definitely my Dream girl, no question about that."

She smiled and I felt her pussy confirm that she felt the same way.

THE MEETING
Office Orgy Story

She was angry when she left the office and got into her car that Friday afternoon. Why her boss was making her go to review business records with a lesser known client she had never met before at 4:00 in the afternoon was beyond her. Since her boyfriend was gone, all she wanted to do was go home, take a warm bath, sign on to her computer, and have a little fun with her new online pal that she had recently met whose words would make her nice and damp and cause her to begin typing with one hand while the other played at the spot that brought her so much pleasure. Instead, she had to go to this stupid meeting. She had to admit that one of the reasons she was mad was not so much that she had to do the work, but that she wanted to go home and play.

Face it, she thought, "You are a horny little bitch and since your boyfriend is not home to give you a good hard fuck, you were hoping for a little online release."

When she arrived at the client's office she learned that it was a small business that did lab analyses for people who wanted to be tested for sexually transmitted diseases. By the time she got to the main business office, most everyone was gone. She was led into a small conference room. There she met Alan, a lawyer, who was one of the investors and appeared to be the leader, Bill who was head of finance, Tony who was from marketing, and Jack who was from operations. As Alan explained what they did, he also mentioned, as an aside, that, as part of the program, everyone who works at their company had to get tested.

With a teasing smile he said, "And, by the way, we all passed with a clean bill of health."

Could he read her mind? Again, she did not know if it was because she was so very horny or something else, but she found all four men very attractive. Alan was in his early 40's, about 5' 8", with beautiful brown eyes, wearing an impeccably tailored suit. Bill was tall and slim with light brown hair, Tony was blond and boyish, and Jack was black, about 5' 10", with caramel colored skin.

Alan started the meeting by stating that, while the business was growing and successful, they were not making any money and they wanted her to review their books and tell them why. While he seemed very pleasant, he was also the leader and was direct and matter of fact. The other men gave him deference. After reviewing some of the materials and answering some of her initial questions, the men left her to review the business documents.

As he was leaving, Alan stated, "We will be down the hall in the lounge watching the basketball game. If you have any uestions, please come down and ask."

After about an hour of reviewing the documents (which should have taken only about thirty minutes, but Candi's mind kept wandering, thinking about what each of the men would be like in bed), Candi went down the hall to ask a few questions. The door was open and the men invited her in. They were watching the basketball game on a big flat screen TV on the wall and drinking beers. Candi sat down on the couch with Alan as the men muted the TV. She could tell he was attracted to her by the way he looked at her and touched her arm when he spoke to her. She asked her uestions and got her answers.

As she was about to leave, Jack asked her if she wanted a beer.

"No, thanks, I am still on the clock, " she replied, "By the way, how is the game?"

Tony said it was a rout and getting boring.

With that, Candi walked back to the conference room. After about another forty-five minutes, she had done all she could do there and needed to take the files back to her office to finish. She packed her materials and went down the hall to tell the men. It was late now and the place was deserted.

Candi walked down the corridor, but, this time, the door was closed. Since they invited her in last time, Candi did not knock, but went right in. To her amazement, the men were no longer watching the basketball game. Instead, on the big flat screen was a beautiful blonde with huge tits that were obviously store bought. However, what she was doing was amazing! This woman was straddling one guy, riding his cock like a sex-starved cowgirl on the range, while another cock was deep down her throat. Also, there was another man behind her, thrusting in and out of her very shapely ass. The woman was moaning deeply, obviously enjoying herself.

Candi was mesmerized by what she saw and did not know how to react. Neither did the men. They were in too much shock to pause it, mute it, or turn it off.

Finally, in what were probably a few seconds, but seemed like hours, Alan spoke up, "Um, uh, sorry, Candi, the basketball game got really boring so we thought we would watch something a little more exciting. I hope we did not offend you. Have you ever seen a porn movie before? You are welcome to watch with us if you want to."

Candi paused, still not knowing how to react. She had seen skin flicks before, but not one quite like this. The image on the screen turned her on very much and she could feel her silk thong start to dampen.

"Can I have a beer?" she asked.

"Sure," Bill replied.

"Come sit by me on the couch and watch the rest of the movie," Alan said.

As Bill handed her a beer and she sat down on the couch next to Alan, she quickly scanned the faces of the other men. They were all too embarrassed to look at her so they kept focusing on the screen. She could tell that all of them had delicious hard-ons, especially Jack, who looked like he had a lead pipe hiding in his pants.

As the scene progressed, Candi sat quietly next to Alan, dranking her beer. The blonde in the film was so lucky, getting fucked like that. She loved watching that cock disappear into her ass and the other cock into her pussy. Her face was getting fucked the same way. Watching this made Candi hot as hell and it was all she could do to stop from reaching down and stroking her own clit.

Soon she realized that Alan had gotten a little closer to her and had his hand on her thigh.

"Are you enjoying this?" he asked.

She turned to him and, as he stared deep into her eyes, she stammered in a whisper, "Yes."

"Me too," he said, "but I am more of a doer than a watcher."

With that, he leaned over and passionately kissed her. Candi kissed back, letting their tongues dance in each other's mouths, seeing Alan's ring and knowing he was married, but feeling that she was beyond all that now. All Candi knew was that she wanted to take the place of that lusty, lucky woman on the screen and that there were four anxious hungry cocks in this room who were probably all too willing to accommodate her.

As he kissed her, Alan slowly began removing Candi's clothes. As he nibbled gently on her neck, he unbuttoned her pink blouse, feeling her beautiful 36D breasts that were aching to be released. Fortunately, her lacy, light pink bra unclasped in the front and soon her big boobs were free. Alan was then licking them and sucking her sensitive, pert nipples as if his life depended on it.

Soon her navy knee-length skirt was unzipped. The porn had been turned off by this time and the other guys were watching Alan and her. Someone had turned on background music, and as Alan helped her off with her light pink silk thong while keeping her light pink matching lace top stockings on, he turned to the other men, "Gentlemen, this lovely lady needs our help, if you would be so kind as to remove all your clothes."

That was all the prompting it took and, as Candi sat there on the sofa in the buff, all four men stripped all their clothes off as fast as humanly possible.

Alan had a nice, thick cock matted in dark hair. Bill's cock was like his build, long and slim. Tony's cock was average. Candi then looked over at Jack. Damn, what a monster!! It had to be at least 9 inches long. All Candi could think about at that moment was how she could not wait to stuff that into her holes. Alan then led Candi to the center of the room and made her kneel. Then all four men circled around her.

Candi was in heaven, lost in complete lust, as she turned round and round, touching, stroking, licking, and sucking each of their rock hard cocks.

They were all delicious and each had a drop of pre-cum on it that she dutifully licked off. Each tasted different and she loved them all. She gagged on Jack's big dick and he backed off a little, allowing her to enjoy just milking the dark head. Her tongue twirled around each shaft, her lips kissed each head, and her throat devoured each of them hungrily. After about 15 minutes of this loving oral action, Alan helped her up to her feet and the men closed in on her.

They pinched and sucked her now rock hard nipples, licked her neck and ears, grabbed her ass, rubbed her swollen clit, and fingered her back door. Fingers were probing her pussy and their musty smell was intoxicating. Candi closed her eyes, melting in orgasmic delight. She could not believe that she already came and no one had been inside her yet.

Soon she was back down on her knees, looking at Alan's delicious cock as it was poised in front of her lips. She opened wide and hungrily swallowed the whole thing. Alan slowly and perfectly fucked her face, allowing her saliva to drip all over his cock as she sucked fervently at it. Then she felt Bill behind her, positioning his cock at her pussy.

Candi backed up a little and wiggled her ass, signaling to Bill that her cunt was aching for his dick.With that invitation, Bill slid his cock into her pussy and, after a few false starts, he and Alan got the rhythm down so that as Alan's cock left her mouth, Bill was impaling her snatch. Back and forth they thrusted into her. Candi was lost in the lust of it all, moaning and whimpering at the same time, as these men fucked her mouth and pussy simultaneously.

Finally, Candi could tell by the urgency of Alan's thrusts that he was about to cum and she was almost at the edge, too!

She started to suck Alan harder as Bill began to rub her clit faster while he thrust his stone hard dick in and out of her wet cunt. Before too long, Candi could not hold it any longer and she screamed, "YESSSS! OH, FUCK ME, YES!" as wave after wave of orgasmic pleasure shook her body.

Her passionate screaming was all that was necessary to push Alan over the edge, as he let out a loud grunt and shot a huge load of cum into her waiting mouth. Candi caught most of it in her mouth while the rest splashed onto her face.

As soon as Alan's cock stopped spewing spunk, Bill let out a whimper and Candi felt his long, slender cock splash the insides of her soaking, wet cunt with his hot sperm.

Before she could catch her breath, Jack and Tony were on the floor with her. Jack laid down and Candi gazed lovingly at his enormous rod, all for her to ride. She squatted over his cock, with her ass facing his face, reverse cowgirl style, as Tony stood in front of her. She held her pussy lips poised over Jack's horse dick and, using her right hand, guided its tip into her waiting, dripping pussy. Fuck, that huge cock felt good! She started to move up and down on his monster without her body actually touching his. The only contact between them was his cock thrusting in and out of her slippery wet hole. After a few minutes of enjoying just part of his big penis, Candi slid her tight vagina all the way down his pleasure shaft as her ass finally met his groin and their skin touched for the first time since he entered her.

Just like the woman in the video, she then proceeded to ride his gigantic dick faster and harder like a horny cowgirl while Tony fed her his cock. Jack had his big hands on her ass, pushing her up and down.

On and on they went, until this time her pussy was filled first by Jack's cock pumping load upon load of sweet spunk into her. This brought Candi to another orgasm, but her screams and moans were stifled as Tony stuffed his meat all the way down her throat, so she would not spill a drop as he fed her his man-juice. Candi rolled off Jack and laid on her back on the floor, panting in pure animal lust. She wanted more cock and nothing but cock. She wanted to stay and get fucked by these four guys all night until she had her fill of delicious dick.

Alan stood above her and said, "Gentlemen, this young energetic lady is amazing! However, there is one part of her we have yet to partake and, if you guys don't mind, I think I will have that for myself."

Candi did not need any coaxing or instructions as she turned over and got on all fours, with her ass jutting up toward Alan. "Fuck it, baby! Fuck my tight ass! I want your cock deep in my butthole!"

Alan wet his fingers with his spit, then got them even slicker by sticking them into her pussy which was wet with her own juices and sticky gooey cum, and began playing with her little, puckered asshole, slowly inserting one, then two fingers.

He withdrew them, stuck them back in her cunt, and then took them back out to massage her asshole again.

"Fuck me in the ass, baby," Candi cooed.

With that re□uest, Alan poised his thick cock at the portal of her back door and pushed the head into her asshole.

"All of it," Candi screamed. "I want more! Fuck my ass, baby!" she pleaded.

On that order, Alan plunged his cock all the way into her ass. At first, he began slowly, with long strokes moving in and out of her ass. Then he picked up the tempo and began furiously fucking her in the ass. Candi pushed her hips back with every stroke to meet the full thrust of Alan's cock and, the instant he reached around and touched her clit, she came hard again.

"Cum all over my ass," she commanded and, with the last loud slap of his balls against her ass, Alan pulled out, spurting streams of cum all over the crack of her ass.

Watching all this hot action made the other three men very, very hard again. Candi was ready, willing, and wanted them all. Bill laid on the floor and she slowly s□uatted onto his cock like she did for Jack. She faced Bill in the typical cowgirl position and let him squeeze her big tits and pinch her pointy nipples. Tony got behind her and, with no more lubrication needed thanks to Alan's wet, sticky spunk, slid his cock easily into her ass. Finally, Jack stood to Candi's right and she grabbed his horse cock and started to lick its swollen mushroom head. He pushed his huge snake further into her mouth and her cheeks puffed in and out while she sucked mightily and hungrily on his dick. The double penetration drove her wild. She had never experienced anything like that before and orgasm after orgasm hit her.

When Jack came, she felt as if a cum faucet had been turned on in her mouth, but she managed to lap up every drop of his tasty sperm. Right after Jack shot cum down her throat Tony came in her ass, pulled out, and shot hot cum on both her cheeks. Jack moved away after his dick had been licked clean by Candi and Tony stood up and backed off after massaging and moisturizing Candi's ass with his cum.

Bill then rolled her over onto her back and climbed on top of her. He pulled her legs up onto his shoulders, slid his entire shaft into her cunt, and started to furiously pound away like a jackhammer. He went at this unbelievable pace for about five minutes when he suddenly pulled out, stood up, and emptied a huge wad all over her tits, face, and hair.

For the next two hours, Candi was enjoying pure hedonistic, lustful pleasure because as soon as one cock shot its load somewhere in her or on her, another stiff one took its place. Candi always had at least one cock in her at any one time, whether it be in her ass, mouth, or pussy. Each men came at least four times and they all had a chance to cum in each of her precious holes. Candi actually lost count of how many times she actually came during the intercourse of the evening. When it was all over, Candi lay on her back on the floor in the middle of the room, exhausted, but very satisfied. She was drenched in cum; it was all over her, in her hair, on her tits, on her face, on her ass, on her legs, and oozing from her pussy and ass.

She badly needed to clean up and Alan led her down the hall to the bathroom where there was a shower.

She was walking with him on very weak legs from all the orgasms she had had during the night's sex session and he was helping her by carrying her clothes and giving her someone to lean on. He left her in the shower and, as she let the warm water wash over her body, she closed her eyes, smiled, and ran through her mind's eye the events that had unfolded and all the wild things she had just done. It made her very hot again and she wanted to touch herself, but her pussy was way too sore.

After she got dressed, she slowly and gingerly walked back down the hall to the lounge. Alan was the only guy left and he escorted her to her car.

"Thank you for such a delightful evening! We all enjoyed ourselves very much! However, I still expect that report to be on my desk by the close of business on Monday."

With that remark, he grinned, gave her a loving pat on her well-ridden ass, and sauntered off.

When Candi got home, she fell into a deep, peaceful sleep. She could not wait to tell her new online friend about her experience, but that would have to wait for another day...

COMFORTING FUN
Group Swinging Story

Feeling a little bored one night I decided to go out. I could have called my usual gang of friends and seen what kind of trouble we could have gotten into but, instead I decided to go solo. There was a new high scale type of lounge that had just opened. I figured it would be a good place to relax, have a few drinks, and see where the night took me.

I entered the establishment wearing my nice and tight black dress. I knew I could turn heads in it since it showed my curves off. It was not long before I noticed that I had several sets of eyes on me. Trying to be as nonchalant as possible, I took my seat at the bar. I ordered my drink and sat there waiting to see what or who would come my way next. A few guys passed by checking me out as they moved along. A couple of other women had entered the lounge after me. I noticed a young blonde that had entered and had become very popular.

After a couple drinks and some not □uite stimulating conversation, I was about to call it □uits. Suddenly the bartender came up to me and handed me another drink. I was confused since I had not ordered another.

I let him know I did not need another and was interested in cashing out. He informed that it was from someone at one of the tables and they had also paid my bar tab. Intrigued, I took the drink and walked towards the table the bartender had indicated. There sat a man and woman having a couple of drinks themselves.

I introduced myself and thanked them for the drink and paying my bill. They introduced themselves in return as Trevor and Maggie and offered me a seat at their table. I graciously accepted the offer and took a seat right across from them. Though we were sitting, I could tell Trevor was tall. He had short, salt and pepper colored hair. His eyes were a piercing blue and his face was clean shaven. Maggie had long black hair. Her hazel eyes popped from the spectacular job of her eye shadow and liner. They were both dressed extremely nice, he in an expensive looking suit and tie and her in a very tight, dark blue dress that looked like she had been poured into.

We sat and talked for a while, all of us sipping on our drink feeling the buzz take over. The way the duo stared at me I was pretty sure I knew what was on their mind.

I started to get excited and was looking forward to this little adventure. An hour or so past and we had decided to leave. I lived close so I told them I was just going to get a cab and head home.

"Oh, that sounds like no fun." Maggie said as we exited the lounge. "Why don't you come home with us?"

I was a little stunned but knew this was exactly what they had intended the whole time. I was planning on playing a little coy but, the alcohol had wiped that plan out and I agreed enthusiastically. Trevor had hailed a taxi for us and we all climbed in. I sat between Maggie and Trevor. The entire short trip to their home, the pair had rubbed my legs and arms trying to get me warmed up for what was to come without getting the attention of the driver. We pulled up to the house and got out. Maggie and I started to walk up the sidewalk while Trevor paid the cab fare. Using her key, Maggie unlocked the door and we went inside.

Shortly after being inside, Maggie grabbed me and planted a huge kiss on my lips. They were super soft, unlike any woman's lips I had kissed before. We pulled close together, wrapping our arms around each other. Still in cuddled together, Maggie guided me towards their bedroom.

Along the way, we discarded unneeded articles of clothing. By the time we entered the room, we were both out of our dresses and topless wearing nothing more than our panties and each other's lipstick. We moved close to the bed, standing at the foot as we continued our make out session. Our hands roamed free, exploring the others body. I was so turned on I felt like a flood could erupt from me at any moment. I heard the sound of the front door opening and closing as the sounds of footsteps echoed getting closer and closer.

Trevor entered the room having already shed his jacket and tie. His shit was unbuttoned and he began to remove it and his undershirt as soon as he entered. He walked up to us now only with his pants on. Maggie broke our kiss as Trevor placed his hands on our exposed backs. We turned out attention to him as he pulled us closer to him. We took turns kissing him. His kisses were much more powerful and dominant that Maggie's.

We stepped back a little and Trevor put his hands on our breasts. He alternated between me and Maggie. We both had reached down to his groin and rubbed his hardening penis from inside his pants. Maggie pulled in close to me and whispered in my ear.

"Feel how hard he is getting?" she asked coyly. "Why don't you get down there and let him free!"

I was so turned on by her bold statement. I lowered myself down to my knees in front of Trevor. I reached for his belt and unfastened the buckle, quickly pulling it apart. I fumbled for a minute with the clasp of his pants before unsnapping it and pulling the zipper down. His cock sprung free. It was big but, not monstrous. I let go of his pants, letting them fall to the floor and wrapped my hands around his phallus. It was still getting hard in my hands as I gently stroked it. I heard the sounds of Maggie and Trevor kissing but, my gaze was laser focused on Trevor's crotch. Lust flooded my mind and instinct took control.

I opened my mouth and wrapped my lips around his dick. I slowly moved up and down his shaft, lightly sucking and swirling my tongue around the head of his cock. I slurped hungrily on him building up speed and taking just a little more of him into my mouth each time. I could hear Maggie kissing her husband as I swallowed his cock. Her hand ran through my hair making that much more excited. In and out, his cock moved from my mouth as my head swam with the ocean of lust inside it.

Maggie lowered herself to her knees besides me and kissed

my cheek. I pulled Trevor's penis from my mouth to take a break. His sigh of disappointment lasted only a second when Maggie continued where I had left off. I watched as she matched my speed and rhythm. Her beautiful full lips moved up and down his shaft for what seemed like eternity. Suddenly she backed off of him and stroked him with her hand. I was mesmerized by her movement. She turned to me and gave me a wink before returning him to her mouth.

I watched as removed her hand and began taking more and more of him into her mouth. I was so turned on. Maggie paused just a moment to look up at Trevor who was in a state of ecstasy I have never seen before. After nearly a minute she pushed her face forward taking all of Trevor into her mouth and throat. Her nose touch his pubic flesh. Trevor groaned from pleasure before Maggie pulled off of him.

She returned to her feet and took my hand. She climbed up on the high bed pulling me with her. We stumbled as we tried to get on the bed, falling into a position with her on her back and me between her legs. Not wasting the opportunity, I spread her legs, removed her panties, and I pulled my face closer in. Her scent was intoxicating. My body moved on autopilot. I reached out with my tongue and licked her soaking wet sex from the bottom to the top. Her juices flowed on to my tongue and down my throat. She tasted even better than she smelled. I greedily lapped at her trying to get every drop of her I could into my mouth. Her moans began to fill the room. I quickly flicked my tongue over her clit. She jumped each time I made contact with it. I could tell the little shocks of pleasure were getting to her.

I suddenly felt a pair of hand on my waist. Trevor had come behind me and pulled my panties down. I shifted so that I was on my knees with my butt sticking towards him. I felt a flood coming from me. I could feel my own juices running down the inside of my thighs. I was beyond turned on. I focused back on Maggie. I pushed my tongue insider her waiting vagina as deep as I could. I flicked it up and down trying to get as much of her essence into my mouth as possible. Trevor had positioned himself behind me and I felt his own tongue on my needing sex. He attacked my clit with his tongue sending shockwaves through me.

I had always had the fortune of being a girl who could climax pretty quick. Trevor's mouth on my pussy was bringing me to my first for the night. Maggie squirmed from my touch as I squirmed from Trevor's. I nearly peaked when he released me from his grip. This broke my concentration on Maggie. I looked up at the beautiful woman. She had her gaze fixed on her husband as he stood behind me. I watched as she simply nodded to him.

I felt his hand on my waist then a familiar poking sensation on my folds. Inch by inch he entered me. I thought he was big from sucking him earlier but he felt so much bigger inside me. I moaned the entire time he pushed his organ inside. He paused when he was fully enveloped inside my body. I panted from the sensation of fullness I now felt.

With both hands on my hips, he began to move in and out. Slowly he pulled himself to the point of nearly being out of me before he pushed back inside. I was in heaven. I could do nothing but moan and sigh. Maggie shifted herself our faces were close together. Seductively she whispered, "Does it feel good?"

I could only nod. A wicked grin came across her face as she shifted her gaze back to her husband. Trevor suddenly slammed himself into me. His pace began to become quicker and more forceful. Like an animal unchained, he fucked me. My first orgasm hit hard. I thrashed on the bed screaming in joy. My sounds only excited him more. Harder and harder he thrusted. A second orgasm hit me and then a third. My body gave out and I collapsed. Trevor's hard cock popped out of me before I fell flat on the bed.

Trevor climbed on the bed between Maggie and I. His cock was still hard as a steel rod. Maggie took the opportunity to position herself over him. Again she looked at me with a wink. She dropped her body strait down on his shaft. He filled her sex instantly and she screamed with delight. She placed her hands on his chest and began to move her butt up and down at a pace that was almost as quick as he had done to me. I could only watch in amazement. His hands grabbed her hips and he began to thrust upwards trying to match her pace.

The duo fucked with a tender yet violent frenzy. My hand had made its way to between my legs as I watched them. Her screams and his moans filled my head. The added sound of their bodies smacking together along with my own moans filled the room. Maggie motioned to me. I moved close and our lips met. WE ferociously kissed each other. Her hand ▢uickly pushed mine away from my wet pussy and began to insert a finger into me. I bucked against her as another orgasm built.

It was just as intense as the previous ones. I thrashed and screamed as I came, drenching her hand in my cum. This pushed her over the edge. She screamed out in bliss as her hips wildly bucked against her husband who was still pounding away at her. Her body shook from pleasure as screamed out obscenities. Trevor's sounds got louder too as his climax approached.

Maggie quickly dismounted him and pulled me down so we were both at his cock. We hungrily licked and sucked knowing he was about to cum in a big way. His cock suddenly erupted and the first blast landed on my face. I stuck my tongue out to get what I could the next one landed on Maggie, running from the bridge of her nose to her chin. Again and again he sprayed us. When he finally finished we took turns giving him a gentle last suck. We were each rewarded with a small amount of his cum in our mouths.

Maggie and I kissed again and licked Trevor's semen off of each other. Once we were both clean, we cuddled up next to him. He gave both of us a long hard kiss before pulling the blankets on the bed over us. There we all fell asleep, worn out from the wild sex that had just taken place. When the morning came, I got dressed. As I left, Maggie kissed me on the cheek. "We will have to do that again soon."

WORKSHOP SESSION

Gangbang Sex Story

It had been too long. I hadn't had sex for over a year, and I was starting to feel deprived. My friend Sarah noticed that. "Girl it's been too long! You need to catch up with me!" She was right. Beautiful, sexy Sarah, fifty- something years young, and she was partying harder and getting more action than anyone else I knew. I was a little more than half her age and still feeling virginal in a lot of ways. I was letting my shyness keep me from getting close to anyone. I had closed myself off for far too long and it was time to open up.

She told me about this workshop, "Exploring Tantric Intimacy". She said her friends have been going for a while and they really enjoyed it. "You could get laid," she said, "like hard core. Really it's about emotional intimacy and stuff like that, but seriously girl, go get you some."

So, I ventured off into the unknown, signed up for the workshop and drove off into the hills to "get me some". The place was gorgeous, with a main lodge, little cabins, hot tubs, greenhouse, gardens, and a winding creek leading to a pond. Dang, I thought. So many places to do it. My nerves started going crazy and I got tingly thinking about the possibilities. What was I in for?

Several hours later I was all signed in. I had no idea what to expect. I was dressed in a long skirt and a sweater, trying to appear demure. Maybe I'll just observe and take notes, I thought. That will be enough. There were icebreakers, Questions and laughter, and then some old guy was lecturing us about love and intimacy, talking about opening chakras and points of sensitivity. Delayed gratification. Prolonged pleasure. Third eye expansion.

I started to tune him out and instead was eyeing the group, picking out the people I wanted to delay gratification with first. There were a few other women, mostly older than me, and a lot of men. Everyone looked lovely to me. I guess I was "softening my aura" as I thought I heard the Instructor say. Or maybe I just knew everyone else was as horny as I was. Yeah, I would sit on that guy's face, even if he is about eighty, I was thinking. I bet he still has it. And probably that lady's as well. I bet she could lick a girl properly, even if she is with that bald dude who's already sporting a semi-boner. I was definitely checking out my options. I spotted a younger man with dark hair, kind of nervous looking. Yum, I thought. An older guy with grey hair and a mischievous twinkle in his eye. Double yum.

I tuned back into the Instructor. He was explaining tantra as a way of connecting deeply in the moment. He spoke about the benefits of prolonging orgasm, how it becomes a full body experience...something about making love to Spirit and honoring Mother Nature with our direct connection to fertile life. I was looking at his white hair, his hands moving through the air as he talked, and I wondered how many orgasms he's had the pleasure of witnessing in his life.

Then I heard him say that the best way to learn is by doing, so we would be breaking into smaller groups for a more intimate lesson. The groups were varied, some were all male, and some had one woman per several men. We each had our own little area. His co- instructors each took a group, and I ended up in the Instructor's group. He took me aside and told me for the purposes of this lesson he needed me to have complete trust and surrender. That I would be blindfolded, lying down, and that he would be giving instructions and guidance during the demonstration. He said everyone here was clean, and that because I was on birth control we would be having "full skin contact", as he called it.

I was getting juicier by the moment, but I kept my demeanor calm. I told him that it all sounded fine. He said I would be in very good hands, that this was a professional and safe environment, and that I could say stop at any time. But I won't want to, he said with a twinkle in his eye. I was in. "Ok if I remain Quiet during the demonstration?" I asked him and he said best if I do. He told me I was a receiver, that I was here to simply allow the body to do what comes naturally. I let him tie the silky blindfold across my eyes and my world went dark.

I had no idea what I was in for. My sex life had been pretty vanilla thus far. Maybe I'll get felt up, I thought, or even finger-banged. That would be exciting! He led me to a large, low table with a thick pad on top. I felt several hands reach out and touch me as I was guided to lie down on my back. I stretched out, feeling a big smile on my face, and then I remembered I was a little geisha doll for their educational purposes, so I tried to calm myself and show no emotion. Let them work for it, I thought.

The Instructor was lecturing in a soft voice, talking about touch receptors, and I felt my clothes being gently tugged off. The room was warm and I felt good, even though I was naked, blindfolded and at the mercy of a group of men. I paid for this, I was thinking. This better be good. I felt hands laying gently on me, touching me lightly everywhere, as the Instructor maintained a rhythmic, verbal manual on How to Please a Woman Properly.

They were massaging me gently, on my feet, neck and shoulders, murmuring about beautiful curves and succulent flesh. I heard the Instructor say that one of the most important things to master was oral stimulation. They would all get a chance, but he needed a first volunteer. I heard some jostling and grunting as they figured that one out. The Instructor was telling them to ease a woman into her pleasure, not rush things. He was holding me open as he explained the anatomy of the vagina, touching lightly, then he was guiding someone's face into my "lotus of a thousand petals", as I thought I heard him call it.

My body gave a jolt as a nice, soft tongue started stroking gently against my thighs and then licking the wetness of my warm, soft "lotus". He was following the Instructor's directions to lick the inside of the labia major, then the labia minor, and then the soft spot below the urethral opening. Then circling the outside of the clitoral hood, while holding back from licking the actual clitoris.

His talk was very anatomical, but the sensations being delivered were incredible. It was like a soul massage, starting with my puss. I heard him say it was time to give someone else a try, and then a new mouth was down there, licking me softly. The instructor guided him around the perineum and vaginal opening, showing him how to stimulate the g-spot, which he called the "fountain of eternal juice", or something like that.

They took turns in this way, licking me as he told them to, being gentle with my clit until it was throbbing with need. Then I felt a finger inside me and a small moan escaped my saliva-drenched mouth. He was telling them to make a "come here" gesture with the finger just inside the vagina, to stimulate the g-spot. They practiced on me, long fingers gently coaxing my body up from the table, come here, their hands were whispering.

"Ok now gently, you want her to get hot but not explosive, go ahead and put your tongue to her clitoris and press softly," he was saying. "Just let it rest there, allowing the pressure to increase as you pull her towards you. "

Whoever was down there was doing a fine job. My clit was on fire, and he was licking it so gently, it felt like heat was oozing over my entire body. I was throbbing everywhere. Now the Instructor was letting them lick me with more pressure, showing them how to treat the ass, the thighs, the breasts, everything. I felt hot mouths sucking my tits, biting my nipples, and I knew I could come in a second, but I wanted to be a good student so I breathed deeply and held it back.

The instructor noticed I was flushed, he told them to ease

back a bit, that I was getting overheated. I heard the rustling of clothing and I imagined that they were getting naked, glistening cocks bobbing out straight and hard as they gathered closer around the table. I felt a hand lift up my head and give me a sip of water, and more hands were massaging my feet and legs. The Instructor was talking about penetration, different angles and techniques to give different sensations. I breathed deep, trying to diffuse the heat rising in my crotch.

I heard him ask for a first volunteer to demonstrate penetration techniques, giving a reminder that the objective was to withhold orgasm for as long as possible, to prolong the pleasure. I was pulsing with anticipation, feeling wetness ooze down between my thighs. I felt the heat of a male body moving on top of me, not making contact with me except for the silky hot tip of his cock, gently stroking my vulva up and down. The instructor told him to insert the head only, staying shallow for ten strokes and then sinking in part way for the next stroke.

I was glad I had been doing a lot of yoga lately, my legs spread apart easily and I felt really limber. The man on top of me was in a kind of push-up position. I couldn't feel his body weight, only the head of his cock, sliding gently in and out of me. It was incredible. I was along for the long ride.

My need to orgasm had faded back a little, now I was just enjoying the sensation of being fucked gently and watched by several guys. How many? I had no idea, I guessed five or six total, but it didn't matter. The Instructor's soothing voice was making me feel safe. This was for education. We were all here for the same reason: to explore our sexuality, to get better at it. To get laid hard core. I wanted to be a willing participant, so I went with whatever was being suggested.

I felt a cock sink into me, only part way, and I let out a soft moan. The man of the moment pulled back and repeated this seＱuence a few times, then it was someone else's turn. Another cock was pressing lightly into my wetness, massaging me, opening me up.

My lotus was feeling good. This time he was allowed to sink his entire length inside of me, after giving me ten shallow strokes. I tried to keep my passive expression, but I couldn't keep from moaning. It felt so good, being filled after being stimulated so much. He held himself inside of me, still, for a few seconds, and then pulled out to give me the shallow strokes again. It was driving me wild.

One after another they took turns. I let myself relax into the pure sensation of it, trying to stay Ｑuiet, trying not to laugh or say anything. The perfect pupil. The Instructor was talking about rhythms, about using the hips to thrust in and upwards, stimulating the clitoris. I felt the cock inside of me growing harder and bigger. I was breathing heavily. The Instructor must have noticed, because he asked the man to step off and let someone else have a chance. He asked me if I was doing ok and I said yes, then I was being filled by another silky, hard piece of goodness. He told him to give me ten shallow thrusts and then a deep hard one, and the man did as he was asked.

It felt like circles of light were moving out of my body, coming out of my crotch and going into space. Soon he was replaced and the next man was allowed to thrust deep and hard into me, in a rhythmic motion. I felt my clit stiffening with desire and the Instructor was telling him to slow down. I suppressed a giggle, thinking that he was saying things I would be saying if I was talking. This old guy knew his stuff!

By this point I was breathing hard and moaning lightly, making a guttural purr. Mouths were sucking on my breasts, tugging lightly at my hair, massaging my feet and pulling my legs wider apart. I heard the instructor say, "Jr. it's your turn, you've got the biggest penis, time to bring her to the Temple of a Thousand Lights. But don't rush it! "

I felt Jr. position himself over me. His body was giving off heat and little droplets of sweat were dripping down onto me. I pictured the young, nervous dark-haired man I had seen before. Here's your chance, I thought. Show them what you're made of! He entered me easily, pushing in about halfway, as the Instructor told him to. He was thick and I could feel him throbbing inside of me. Someone slid a pillow under my ass and then Jr. was thrusting deeper into me. I moved my hips upward and I heard the Instructor tell me to relax, that I was the receiver, I didn't have to work for this one. Tantra was about the journey, he said.

It was sweet agony. My body was slippery, my clit was on fire, but all I could do was lay there and take it. Jr. was doing a pretty good job of giving it to me. I could hear the sound of skin being slapped and I pictured them all with their dicks in their hands, stroking furiously. I started to slip into another realm as Jr. pounded into me. I was crying out a little bit each time, clenching my fists, and the men held my hands so that I had something to squeeze.

I heard the Instructor tell him, "Upwards! Pull her towards you with your Wand of Power!" and then Jr. was pushing hard inside me while his pelvis was pulling up, rubbing against my clit. My body was being pulled into the air by his huge cock. It was the perfect feeling. I reached out for him, and I could feel his silky hips and muscular ass, slick with sweat.

Jr. was grunting with the effort, and I heard the other guys saying things like "Yeah, do it, give it to her hard" and then Jr. was doing it. His cock swelled inside me, shoving even harder into the depths of me and I cried out loudly, moaning "Uhhhh!" He was pushing up inside me and I let myself go there with him, with everybody, judging from the sounds I was hearing in other parts of the building. Little cries and moans were rising, like an orgasmic symphony. I put my arms out to my sides, spreading my knees and lifting my feet into the air.

The waves of pleasure intensified as Jr. pushed hard and fast into me, and I could not hold back any longer. It felt like he was fucking my soul. My clit throbbed with tension as he rubbed himself against me and then it exploded. The throbbing took over my entire body as his hot, sticky juice released inside of me. The shockwaves continued, it felt like my orgasm was lasting forever. I was moaning uncontrollably, then I felt Jr. pull out and another dick was soon inside of me, big and hard and pushing into me forcefully.

I moaned loud and opened my legs wider. I heard grunting and I knew without a doubt that it was the Instructor. He moved with so much force and finesse that within moments my orgasm returned and exploded again with waves of pleasure moving over my body and out into the world. I couldn't stop shaking. He squirted inside of me and moved off, then I felt loads of hot juice rain down on me. I spread my arms wide in surrender and they showered my face, breasts and belly, bathing me in warm silky rivers of "liquid life force", as the Instructor had been calling it.

I lay there breathing heavily, and within a few moments it was quiet. I felt a warm, damp towel on my face, wiping gently, then wiping my body, taking time between my legs. I heard the Instructor say in a soft voice that I had performed excellently, and to take my time getting up. There was a private shower I could use, and then I was dismissed for the rest of the afternoon. I could lie down and rest, if I wanted to. Maybe soak in the hot tub or stroll in the gardens.

I said thank you. He asked if I enjoyed it. I said yes, very much. Exquisite, really. I felt his fingers brush over my fur and I trembled. Then they were inside of me, playing lightly with my clit, slipping easily over the smooth, wet softness, and then sliding deep inside of me. Come here, they said. I □uivered, instantly wanting to be pounded again until I passed out from total exhaustion. "What do you think?" he asked, "You feeling up for a quickie?" I remembered his thick cock buried inside of me, and I knew I was up for anything.